ASSASSINATION!

The pilot of the chopper waiting for his passengers spotted the fleeting figure of Bodie. The pilot did not hesitate, surprised though he was. He pulled his gun, leaned from the canopy and opened fire on Bodie.

Bullets ripped into the gravel before Bodie's feet. He dived and rolled and came up in the aim and shot at the chopper. Bullets pranged.

But the group around Ojuka and Avery scattered and now the henchmen were shooting at Bodie. Gunfire broke shatteringly against the sky . . .

Also by Ken Blake in Sphere Books:

THE PROFESSIONALS
Foxhole

KEN BLAKE
Based on the original screenplays by
Brian Clemens and Dave Humphries

SPHERE BOOKS LIMITED
30–32 Gray's Inn Road, London WC1X 8JL

First published in Great Britain by
Sphere Books Ltd 1982

Novelization copyright © Sphere Books 1982

**TRADE
MARK**

Set in Photon Baskerville

Printed and bound in Great Britain by
Cox & Wyman Ltd, Reading

Chapter One

Jack Cobber went to a lot of trouble to welcome Roddy Barker out after twenty-five years. That was a long time, far worse by more than the apparent five years that Cobber had done. Cobber heard the door bell ring and he braced himself to meet Roddy Barker again.

The apartment was nice, on the open plan, and Maisie had made it very comfortable. Cobber moved to the door and opened it. He was around fifty, a jittery, nervous man and a fussy dresser. His old associates knew that the fire had gone out of him, though, over the years.

Not so Roddy Barker. He was about the same age as Cobber; but he looked hard and rugged, a certain greyness about his face giving him a lean and predatory look, and he was a man tensed with nervous energy who knew exactly what he wanted.

The fire had not gone out of Roddy Barker.

They shook hands, and then Cobber half-turned, and speaking as though making an announcement, said: 'Roddy Barker.'

They moved out of the vestibule into the lounge, and the place came alive. It had appeared empty, quiet and restful and just what Barker wanted. Suddenly, Cobber's wife Maisie, a number of men and women all smiling and extending their hands, jumped out from where they had been hiding. They all welcomed Roddy Barker back, calling greetings, saying how glad they were to see him. The air filled with noise. Cobber beamed.

They surrounded Barker, women giving him wet kisses, men thumping his shoulder. They wanted him to feel back home.

Barker shook his head. He looked bewildered.

'No . . .' he whispered.

'Thought you'd appreciate some *real* company at last,' said Cobber, laughing with pleasure.

'No . . .'

Cobber began to look bewildered.

'Come on, Roddy – '

'I didn't want this. I don't want this.'

The people suddenly fell silent. They moved back a little, giving Barker space, all staring at him. He licked his lips. He shook his head, much as a bull shakes his head in the ring.

'Not now,' he said. 'Not yet. I'm not ready yet.'

Maisie, high-coloured, cheerful, spoke up. 'Roddy – '

'I know what I want, Maisie. And I don't want this.'

He moved, suddenly, hunching his shoulders and turning his back on the company. Cobber anxiously moved closer.

'Get rid of 'em, Jack. *Just get rid of them!*'

The embarrassment of the crowd caught at Jack Cobber. But he sensed that he'd better do as Barker wanted. He turned to the people, a little flustered, a little upset, not quite sure what Roddy Barker was about but very sure that he'd better do as Barker said. 'Whatever you say,' he said, and shooed the people away.

A young man with a deal of dark bristle about his chin and a short hairstyle came up to Roddy Barker. He touched Barker on the arm.

'You're an ungrateful bastard. Jack put a lot of time on this – '

Quickly, smoothly, suddenly, Barker pivoted and hit the young man on the chin, knocked him staggering back across the room. He stood over the sprawled man, looking down, and the tension in Barker appeared a tangible force. The young man was suddenly very frightened.

Barker looked once, then pivoted again and walked into the adjoining room. Cobber helped the young man to his feet. He brushed him down. 'Don't take it personal, son. He put in a lot of time, too. And after twenty-five years hard – he needed to hit something.'

Maisie and Jack Cobber let Barker sleep in, as they thought, but when the dawn was still a pale smudge of reddish grey over the London skyline, Jack Cobber found Barker leaning against the high balcony parapet. Barker was staring moodily over that impressive skyline, with the towers and tower blocks, the chimneys and smoke stacks lifting from the shadowed jumble of buildings below. A tang on the morning air blew refreshingly, high above the smoke.

Barker half-turned as Cobber crossed to him, and then resumed that intent scrutiny across the rooftops.

'It's not so hot,' he said.

Cobber looked askance at this.

'The Moor, Princeton, Exeter,' Barker went on. 'I used to dream about that view. Yet it's not so hot. No, I don't miss it.'

Cobber made an attempt to chivvy Barker out of this black mood.

'You going away, Roddy?'

'That's what we promised ourselves, wasn't it, Jack?' Barker's words were low, ruminative. 'I remember . . . Us lying there beside the tracks, waiting for that train. You, me, Benny, Terry. South America we promised ourselves.'

'Benny made it.'

'Yes. That lucky Benny. Kept his share, too. But us? You a twenty. Me a twenty-five. Terry knifed and dead in a prison yard brawl. And not a cent to share between us.'

Barker turned, abruptly, staring with dark meaning upon Cobber.

'They owe us, Jack!'

Cobber shook his head.

'That's not good talk.'

'Only thing that kept me sane.'

'Roddy . . . You so much as *sniff* at another train – or a bank – or a payroll – '

'Nothing like that.' Strength rode in Barker's words.

3

'New line altogether. Nothing they can ever link to us.'

Cobber stared at Barker, seeing him as it were afresh, in a new light. He wasn't sure that he cared for what he saw; but they were mates . . .

'Not *us*,' he said. 'Not us. I did my twenty. I couldn't do another week.'

'But Jack –'

'Not another hour! It'd kill me.'

Barker took a breath. He sounded hard. 'This is *certain* – '

'So was the train robbery. I'm sorry, Roddy.'

For a long moment Roddy Barker looked at his old mate, and saw in Cobber things he had never expected to see. He realised that there was no point in going on. He nodded his head.

'Maybe it's best. No old contacts, nothing to trace back to me. But keep your eye on the headlines, Jack . . .'

He smiled, widely, and yet the strength of purpose in him radiated a palpable force.

'You're going to see me pick up a million, and say to yourself: "That could have been me." '

Bodie walked across to Ray Doyle who waited for him by the wreck of the barrier. The RAF Regiment camp had been raided in the muted shadows of dawn, and a wildly-driven truck had smashed out through the barrier. Bodie caried a piece of paper in his hand. His smooth, dark good looks contrasted with the ruffled appeareance of Doyle as they met by their car.

Doyle gestured around the camp, indicating the perimeter fence, the guardhouse, the smashed barrier. He looked at Bodie.

'It was an inside job. Op. as smooth as that, they had to have an inside man.'

'Yeah,' said Bodie.

'We'll run through all the names.'

Bodie looked disgusted.

'That'll be fun.' As Doyle looked up quickly, his partner went on: 'Know what the strength of this camp is? Over two thousand. Not including civilian staff, or inductees for training, or taking into account they frequently use the place for dispersal. Rough guess I'd say about thirty thousand names pass through this camp every year.'

They turned as Bodie reached Doyle and walked across to the car. Doyle began to get an idea of what Bodie was digging at. They worked as a team for CI5, and they were a good team, even the big man, Cowley, George Cowley, who ran CI5, the Squad, the Big A, admitted they were a good team – every now and then in an unguarded moment.

Doyle jerked a thumb at Bodie's list.

'Box of grenades plus launcher – ?'

Bodie lifted the paper.

'Two machine carbines. Four pistols. One machine gun. And one truck.'

'Lot', said Doyle in a musing way, 'of room in that truck.'

Bodie nodded.

'And a hell of a lot more weapons in the armoury. Weapons which they left behind.'

'They took just enough for one specific job.'

'Yeah.'

They looked at each other, visualising grenades being launched and machine carbines stuttering death. They did not need to be told the seriousness of this situation.

'But', said Doyle, thinking on beyond those visions of death and destruction, 'which job?'

'And', added Bodie, 'where?'

The stolen RAF truck, loaded with sudden death in the form of guns and grenades, stood with its tailgate down in the corner of the abandoned warehouse. Dust hung in the air, and a few lamps threw oddly-shaped shadows. The three men carried the stolen weapons as though they knew how to use them.

Young Stacey, good-looking, lean of jaw, with a wildness about him that had checked bigger men's unpleasant intentions towards him, dumped a box of grenades. He wiped the back of his hand across his forehead and glanced across at Dunstan.

Dunstan was staring at the workbench, under the light. On the bench a few crudely made cardboard models stood like a model fort complex. Cereal packets and soap powder cartons had been cut up to shape and positioned.

Dunstan affected a pair of moustaches wider than the common run. His face bore lines of experience he, at least, wished were never there. He wore smart clothes of a conservative cut, and anyone would see nothing strange in encountering him at the local golf club.

Roddy Barker, hard, authoritative, looked up from the models on the workbench and spoke to Stacey.

'How about the sandbags?'

'Nearly crippled myself lugging 'em onto that roof.'

Barker nodded. 'All covered up?'

'Yeah.' Stacey moved his hand in a circling gesture, flat over the workbench. 'Old tarpaulins and a load of debris.'

'Good.' Having checked with Stacey, Barker turned to his other accomplice. 'Dunstan – you set?'

'Yes.'

'The new paint job?'

'Is in hand.' Dunstan wasn't fool enough to show impatience at this minute questioning – not with Roddy Barker. He jabbed a forefinger at a small black box, its top adorned with switches and buttons, and at the two R/T sets at the side. 'Jammer – good for about a mile radius. Transmitter – receiver – '

'You find a radio frequency?'

'Yes. It's a narrow band; but they're both locked in to the same frequency.' Here Dunstan betrayed the pride he felt at his own skill in the job. 'I taped the dials into position.'

Barker looked pleased. 'Good.' He picked up the transmitter and hefted it. 'We'll only use this once. One code call – '

'Jackpot.'

'Jackpot. That's right.' Now a sense of that aura of controlled violence about Barker made the other two snap up straighter. Barker was into this thing with everything he had, and if his accomplices fouled up – well, better not to think of that.

'Soon as you hear that,' Barker told them, 'You'll – '

' – Come running,' Dunstan finished for him. 'Figuratively speaking.'

'That's fine.' Barker's hard grainy face showed an equally hard grainy smile. 'Fine.' He stared at the other two, a challenging, demanding, bracing stare. 'Tomorrow morning, then. We hit tomorrow!'

As he spoke he touched the crude cardboard model on which they had planned their moves.

The next morning they looked not on the cardboard model of their target but on the bricks and mortar of the building itself.

The block was large, imposing, laced with windows and of that particular greyish colour that London Yellow bricks turn after years of weathering the air of the metropolis.

It was, like a deal of the property on this side of the river, due for demolition to make way for office blocks of sheer glass walls, towering, high, looking contemptuously down on the spires and angled roofs of a previous time. It was, now, still the tallest building around, and it dominated its surroundings. A short way off a factory chimney towered up higher, and the hospital lifted its serried windows nearly to the same height as the old warehouse. But the block stood four square, hard and grey and grainy, like the man who led up the stained concrete stairs.

They had cut the chains on the gates, driven their own van in, and now they were hefting the boxes up to the roof.

Barker and Stacey struggled to haul the stuff up the stairs. The ancient lift with the folding iron gates was a museum piece, and wouldn't work even if there was power on, even if they'd cared to try.

Barker and Stacey had two cases each on carrying straps around their shoulders, and they lugged another case each and a holdall. They were bowed down like Pilgrim's donkeys. They huffed and puffed up the stairs and took stops for breathers. Stacey had to stop on the landing with the wide emergency door to one side leading to stairs outside. The other door across the landing was closed. This door led into the level of the warehouse floor they had reached, and Stacey looked up, and licked his lips, and thought they weren't anywhere near high enough yet.

He picked up the case again, hitched the two over his shoulder, ready to start on up after Barker.

The light here was dim enough to make the dust appear mere concrete, shafting down from above. Stacey felt one case over his shoulder start to slide and he knew the damn thing would slip right off if he couldn't get his shoulder back in time. He tried to jerk himself straight and the holdall tangled, he fumbled it, trying not to drop it and the case over his shoulder held – just. He drew a ragged breath. The holdall gaped open and he'd dropped a damned ammo clip.

He couldn't leave the thing there, on the stairs, Roddy Barker would go mad.

Starting all over again, Stacey lowered the case and holdall, reached for the dropped clip, stuffed it back into the bag, and then, with a fresh grasp on the handles, began to climb up. He was sweating. He panted. He'd made enough noise to alarm a herd of sleeping elephants.

This dusty old place really got down into a man's lungs.

The last flight of stairs leading to the roof were steep. The trapdoor at the top let a flood of light down onto the treads and the dust. Stacey and Barker emerged onto the flat roof and dumped their loads. They took deep dragging lungsful of air.

The first thing Barker did was look all around the horizon, over the rooftops, just like a U-boat commander coming to the surface and taking his three-sixty degree sweep to spot Sunderlands or destroyers. From back here only the pencil thin tip of the factory chimney broke the background of sky and cloud.

Barker nodded, satisfied, and jerked his thumb at Stacey.

That young man bent to the cases and started to open them.

The guns were in there, broken down for transport. There was plenty of ammo. The launcher looked somehow ugly and yet beautiful, a thing designed to do an ugly job yet beautiful because it did a job well.

Bundled into one case was a pile of clothing and a blonde wig. The loose ammo clips – here Stacey wet his lips and cast a furtive glance at Barker – were quickly stuffed back into the holdall.

Barker walked across and picked up a machine carbine, snapped it up. He held it, or so Stacey fancied, with a conscious realisation of the picture he made. A hard, tough man, determined and ruthless, carrying a gun – a gun he'd use without compunction.

Then, moving with a snap, Barker used his free hand to slam the solid steel lid of the trap shut.

The trapdoor lid crashed closed with a heavy, resonant ring.

The two men were cut off on their roof, up there against the sky with an arsenal of weaponry, with sandbags and corrugated iron, with flak jackets and radios, with food and drink – and, over-riding all those things, they were up there against the sky with a purpose they'd use those guns to achieve.

In the open, dusty, deserted space beyond the emergency door a bundle in one untidy corner stirred as though life existed here. When Stacey dropped the ammunition clips the bundle jerked. The folds of cloth rippled. Then a tousled head poked out of the double sleeping bag.

The face was gaunt, bearded, not too clean. Sleeping rough made ablutions difficult.

A battered rucksack to one side and a litter of open cans, a couple of plates and spoons, a pile of newspapers, testified to the hard life.

As the bearded man looked out blearily, listening to stumbling and clattering sounds beyond the door, another

9

head abruptly poked up out of the sleeping bag at his side.

'What is it?' she demanded in a sleepy, irritable voice. Her hair straggled, and her eyes were too dark around the edges, rings within rings; but she was pretty enough, with a few pimples and spots around her nose and chin all the rotten ointments never seemed to shift.

'Shh – '

Stifling a yawn, the man climbed out. He was wearing a T-shirt and jeans. He started off towards the door.

The girl called: 'Bob?'

'Shh,' Bob snapped. 'Hold it down, Sal. Don't forget, we're trespassing.'

She watched him go, and then started to run her fingers through her tangled hair. Men! They said all they wanted was what they always wanted, and then got up and started prowling around nasty abandoned warehouses.

Bob started cautiously up the stairs. The sounds he had heard not only aroused his curiosity, they also alarmed him. Finding a bed for the night was hard enough as it was.

He looked up. His foot hit something hard, which skittered across the dimly lit landing. At once his heart leaped into his mouth. He looked down.

When he bent and picked up the metal clip and the brass and silver cartridges, he recognised this as a clip of bullets. Then a clang sounded above. He started up again, clutching the ammo clip.

At the top he saw a bright rectangle of light, flooding the stairs with radiance. He blinked.

Then, against that brilliant rectangle he saw the unmistakable silhouette of a man holding a gun. The rifle poked up arrogantly.

Abruptly, the lid of the trapdoor came down with a smashing clang.

The noise reverberated in Bob's head. He felt the ammunition clip in his hand, hard and ridged. He swallowed.

Then, silently – very very quietly indeed – he crept down the stairs and back to Sal.

CI5 Headquarters alerted the partners just as Bodie was buying a paper to see what was running.

Doyle, at the wheel of the car, beeped the horn before the R/T finished squawking.

Bodie appeared at the door of the newsagents, juggling paper and coins. Doyle beckoned.

A couple of flung coins and Bodie hared for the car. Doyle swerved her away from the kerb, tyres screeching, before Bodie slammed the door.

'Enderfield Street,' Doyle told his partner the news from HQ. 'Man with gun.'

Approaching Enderfield Street both men were struck by the sudden shabbiness of this little area, so close to modern apartment blocks, and the river, and the hospital, and new shopping precincts. Fast though Doyle drove, to paraphrase a famous cigarette lady, Cowley drove faster. His polished Rover three and a half slewed to a stop inches before Doyle's Escort.

They wasted no words.

George Cowley, head of CI5, a man of unblemished integrity and of ruthless hewing to a purpose, ran the Big A to combat crime. That was what CI5 was all about. They fought criminals with the criminals' own dirty weapons. If they took in a couple of KGB jobs along the way, maybe that was because Cowley had headed up MI5 and had been brought in by special fiat from the PM, the Home Secretary, and other interested parties, to form CI5 along similar lines.

Now Cowley nodded briskly to his two star agents, his upper lip curling, his jaw going in. He wore a light-grey topcoat, rather on the short side, and with a velvet collar rather on the flashy side. His sandy hair, thinning now, was still defiantly riffling in the breeze. Bodie's dark hair sleeked down, slick and trim after his haircut. Doyle's hair just stood up and waved to all the passers by.

Inspector Newton, a craggy dyspeptic man in civilian clothes, waited for them at the doorway of the warehouse.

The big bulky form of Sergeant Wood in his blue uniform added the required touch of authority any person unfamiliar with undercover work would need.

Bob and Sal sat on the steps, looking glum.

They'd done their duty, what Bob wanted to do, and now they were surrounded by coppers. To name them in no other more unflattering way. It wasn't as if Bob and Sal were dregs of society; just they were short of the readies and needed to sleep rough for a bit.

Inspector Newton put his hands on his hips aggressively and fronted up to the chief of CI5.

'Mr Cowley.'

Cowley ignored all that. 'Inspector. You said a gunman.'

Newton nodded his head sideways at the pair on the steps.

'He'll tell you.'

The way the Inspector said that implied that they knew what would happen if Bob didn't tell them . . .

Cowley swung his head.

'Well?'

Bob slowly climbed to his feet. He did look a wreck, and he knew it. He felt uneasy.

'About an hour ago – Sal and me were asleep – '

Newton, belligerently, broke in: 'Illegally trespassing in the building.'

'We didn't break in,' protested Bob. 'There's several windows busted in around the back – '

Newton, very sarcastic with it, said: 'But *you* didn't bust 'em?'

'No – '

Sal stood up, feeling bitter. Her lips twisted.

'I told you. We should have just split and run.'

Cowley realised he'd better keep talking to the man, this Bob. He kept his voice neutral, but sharp. 'What did you see?'

'Man on the roof. I only got a glimpse; but he was carrying a gun.'

'You sure?'

'Well, I wouldn't have been, except – ' His glance swung

12

uneasily sideways to take in Newton. Newton stepped forward, holding out his hand.

'He found this on the stairs.'

The ammo clip was now secreted in a transparent plastic bag, all neatly docketed. Cowley took the bag and held it up. The brass of the cartridge cases shone, the bullets looked menacingly lethal. He held it out.

'Bodie!'

Bodie took the bag, looked at the ammo clip. He was accounted an expert on anything to do with rifles, up to and including wrapping them around the necks of villains. The ammo clip was not quite right for a rifle, not quite –

Bodie said to Bob: 'He was carrying a rifle?'

'Looked like a rifle – '

Bodie cut in, convinced. 'But a thicker barrel?'

'Yes – '

Bodie passed the ammo clip in its plastic bag back to Cowley. When he spoke, the curl in his lips was very marked, a pronounced downward curl of distaste.

'Machine carbine.'

Cowley got rid of the evidence and then he, followed by the others, stepped away from the entrance and the stairs and looked up. As ever, the sense of looking up at a tall building hard against the sky conveyed the impression the building was falling on your head. The party adjourned to the entrance again.

'Have you been up there?' demanded Cowley.

Inspector Newton looked hurt. 'It's twelve floors, but, yes, we've been up there. As far as the door to the roof. It's shut. A steel door.'

Ray Doyle said: 'And you left it at that, did you?'

Newton spoke with a sneer. 'The small print. You boys are always quoting the small print in your authority. Leave it to CI5. So I did.' He stuck his fists on his hips in that aggressive, head-thrust-forward pose. 'I am. And, in this case, I'm glad to!'

Cowley simply half-turned his head and stared at Doyle. 'Doyle?'

'Get our flak jackets and go up there.'

'Bodie?'

'If there is a man up there, I'd like to know why. What area does he command from up there?'

Cowley agreed with this.

Newton said: 'It doesn't overlook Buckingham Palace if that's what you mean.' He gestured around. 'More warehouses, hospital, factory, playing fields, some houses – nothing to write home about.'

Cowley swung back to Bodie, the unspoken question perfectly plain. Bodie wrinkled his lips.

'Like Doyle said. Flak jackets – and let's get up there!'

They didn't waste time fetching their flakjaks but they didn't rush as though their pants were on fire. This was a man-on-the-roof routine with the added man-with-a-gun twist. They'd done it before. If this nutter didn't kill them they'd do it again. As they took out their handweapons – they'd recently turned over to using revolvers again – both Bodie and Doyle once again knew they weren't in the job for money. You couldn't really pay a man enough to go out and get himself killed – when the kings and queens of history had tried that, the hired mercenaries got together and organised battles on a civilised plan. It was known and it was surely done; paying a man to risk his life in a fight. But CI5 meant far more than merely that. George Cowley had spelled it out, and the people he chose for the Big A were the best. The Squad did the job because the job had to be done.

Near the top floor of the dusty stairway Bodie stopped.

He leaned against the wall.

Doyle halted and looked down, smiling.

'Out of condition?' The mockery carried an edge of concern.

Bodie shook his head.

'Good sense. If there *is* someone up there – we don't want to arrive breathless – do we?'

Doyle saw the sweet sound sense in this, and he stopped and took a breather, leaning against the wall, too.

Rifles and revolvers, guns of all descriptions, were odd

and strange products of man's ingenuity. They were merely things of metal and wood and plastic and explosive. The finger on the trigger was what mattered. Anyone who had anything at all to do with guns should be rigorously trained, leaned on. To leave a loaded weapon lying about for a kiddy to find and then shoot another child in a CI5 game was criminal lunacy. And, of course, as soon as a baby in a cot was given a plastic gun as a toy – some toy! – he or she should be told never, ever, point a gun at anybody unless you want to kill them.

The two CI5 agents, guns in their fists, padded up the last flight of stairs towards the trapdoor. They knew how to handle weapons; more importantly, they knew how not to abuse the power weapons conferred.

Roddy Barker's knowledge of guns had been gained in the furtive back alleys and billiards halls, the waste dumps and bomb sites. He sat behind the pile of sandbags on the roof and squinted down the sights of the machine gun. It was a standard NATO GPMG, and it would cut a person in half if you handled it right.

Stacey went on piling up the sandbags and arranging the corrugated iron roof for more. He appeared to be happy in his work. Roddy Barker was exulting in his.

He looked along the line of sight and moved with a finicky precision, getting it just right. He smiled that hard grainy smile.

The sights of the machine gun lined up, and the muzzle pointed at the big picture windows of the hospital.

Barker could see everything in the ward opposite with pinpoint clarity.

He could see the beds and their white linen and red blankets, the drip-feeds, the shining equipment, the record charts. He could see the crisp white uniforms of the nurses as they moved among the six patients, giving them constant attention. He could see the flowers. He could see it all, could Roddy Barker, and he could see it all through the sights of a machine gun.

He licked his lips.

Then, checking, he turned back to Stacey who had finished up with the sandbags. He came back from the steel trap door.

'All secure?'

Stacey gave a small affirmative gesture with flat hands. 'Like Fort Knox up here.'

'Then,' said Barker, 'let's get this show on the road.'

His finger squeezed the trigger. He knew how to do that, did Roddy Barker. His forefinger closed on the trigger and the machine gun began to do the work for which it had been designed. From the muzzle spat flame and smoke and a lethal stream of bullets.

Bodie and Doyle stared up at the closed trap door.

Without words the partners went through the drill.

Doyle took his handgun into both fists and aimed it up. Bodie ran fleetly up the stairs, silently, bent to listen at the trap. His face drew down in concentration. He could hear nothing. He tried the door, felt it resist, tried the lock, felt the tightness. He shook his head and rejoined Doyle.

'Locked firm.'

Doyle eyed the door with that sideways nod of head and flick of eyes. 'Lock's just about – there – right? Maybe the two of us could blast it.'

Bodie nodded. They both took up the shooting stance, aiming at the lock. Their fingers tightened on the triggers.

Then Doyle checked and took his left hand from the butt, and brought out the R/T handset. He spoke in a whisper.

Cowley's voice answered. 'Come in – '

'Someone's up here all right. Door's jammed on the other side. We're going to try to blast the lock.'

'Right.'

With that settled, the partners could get on with it.

Again they took up the stance, fists firm on gun butts. The triggers inched back –

The blast of noise from the trap, the hysterical blattering of a machine gun, shocked them rigid.

16

Instinctively, they flattened against the walls.

But no one was shooting at them.

The machine gun ripped out a long burst.

Bodie and Doyle unfroze. They rushed up the stairs, pouring shots at the trapdoor lock.

For a moment Barker stopped shooting. He turned a snaggle-toothed grin towards the door. Stacey smiled.

'No chance!' he said, proud of his part in the scheme. Sandbags piled on the trap door held it firm; whoever was shooting down there wouldn't blow that trapdoor in a month of Blue Moon Sundays.

At that moment the Intensive Care Unit carried six patients and the ward looked like a highly complex scientific laboratory. The idea of flowers in here appeared incongruous; but there were flowers. Whoever heard, considered Nurse Rutley, of a hospital ward without a nice bunch or two of flowers?

The six women were all fighting for life. They could be saved, given the concentrated concerned care they were receiving. The drip feeds dripped, the monitors monitored, the charts were scrupulously kept up to date, and the nurses and assistants were ready to jump at the first sign of trouble.

This ward cared for those who had successfully lived through the main Intensive Care Unit, and in here Nurse Rutley and her sister nurses brought the people back to life. But they still had to be looked after. Without constant care their lives stood in danger. Nurse Rutley knew that. She knew it very well.

The noise was at first so loud and shattering she just didn't understand it. It was shocking. The whole length of the picture windows just simply exploded. They flew inwards. Glass sprayed everywhere. And the noise went on and on.

Young Nurse Gladys Tomkins fell on the floor, her hands over her ears, her blonde hair a quivering mass, her body jerking, screaming, screaming. . . . Mrs Johnson tried

17

to throw herself out of her bed and tangled herself in her saline feed.

Bits of wall, plaster and tiles, fell down on the inside wall. There was an indescribable noise of buzz saws slicing away. The ward was being cut to pieces.

Nurse Rutley, on the floor, shaking, looked up.

She realised some maniac was shooting a machine gun through the windows, smashing them, spraying the far wall with bullets. They were shooting high. The bullets hit the wall well above the bed level.

She couldn't stand up.

Then, like a clap of thunder, the shooting stopped.

Only the screaming continued.

Doctor Ramsey appeared in the ward. He hauled up, his white coat flying around his legs. His face expressed astonishment. Then outrage. He saw the shambles. He couldn't tell if anyone had been hurt; but if he didn't reach his patients they wouldn't receive the attention they needed.

He started off along the floor.

The dreadful machine gun started up again and bullets hissed through the gaping holes in the wall that had once contained picture windows. Doctor Ramsey dropped to the floor – he fell to the floor. He stared appalled.

He could not walk through a curtain of death.

He could not reach his patients.

Cowley called frantically into his handmike and felt relief when Doyle's voice came back.

'We're okay.'

'What – ?'

'Short of a bomb we can't move the door. He's up here to stay.'

Bodie stared malevolently at the steel door.

'Yeah. Trapped up here.'

Cowley said: 'Come on down!'

Inspector Newton brought the report. He it was who knew where the bullets from the machine on the roof had gone. Cowley brushed aside the disbelief. So a madman was shooting at the hospital. So CI5 would have to stop him.

Simple.

'Seal off the area. Evacuate everyone until we know what this is all about.'

He ran off towards the hospital, his sandy hair riffling, his face hard and determined, set, as hard and determined as the face of the man on the roof.

When Cowley, brushing aside red tape, reached the stricken ward, he found the Doctor trying to stand up, and not being able to do so as bullets slashed above him.

Cowley saw the doctor's dilemma.

'Come back.'

'But,' said Dr Ramsey, helplessly. 'I can't – '

'Back.'

The authority wielded by George Cowley was not simply that conferred by a title, or responsibility, or office. When he said jump, his own innate authority made people jump.

Doctor Ramsey, obediently, crawled back.

They stood up, together, and looked at the wreckage.

'For God's sake – my patients. They are all post-op.'

'There won't be any more shooting – not unless you try to get to them.' Cowley would not let Ramsey interrupt. 'I know – post-op – they need constant care. How long do we have?'

'I – I don't know. Not long.'

'Listen to me. . . . Listen! My name is Cowley. CI5. *I need your help!*' Cowley spoke directly into the ward.

At these words the sounds of crying diminished as the frightened women patients listened to what was being said. Cowley looked as much at the patients as at Ramsey as he spelled out just what was needed.

'There is a man across the street with a gun. He does not mean to harm you. If he did, he could have done that already.'

Cowley looked at the bullet-pocked walls, all the marks high enough to show the truth of what he had deduced.

He went on: 'He wants to shock us, and unfortunately you too. Your doctor here tells me that it is very important that you remain calm. At the moment we cannot get medical aid to you. So, wherever possible, you must help yourselves.'

The women listened intently, helpless in their beds.

'We are doing all we can, and we will have this man out of the way as soon as possible. Meanwhile, listen carefully to the doctor and the nurse here. They will give you instructions for your own care. For self help.'

Cowley did not believe the women patients were totally helpless. They just had to help themselves for the time being. He turned to Ramsey and spoke in a lower tone.

'Get them all doing something, anything. Keep them occupied.'

Cowley gave a curt little nod, turned, and stalked away. He had work to do on the outside.

Doctor Ramsey looked after him. He swallowed.

Then he put a hand through his hair, pulled his white coat straight, and turned to look into the ward.

He spoke briskly, as though merely giving orders in a simple routine matter.

'Mrs Culbert – your drip feed. The line is twisted. Can you readjust that? Just reach over and straighten the line. Good. Mrs Wescott – '

He was moving into the swing of it now, caring by remote control.

CI5, also, was swinging into its organisational stride.

Inspector Newton stood with Bodie and Doyle as the first contingent of CI5 operatives arrived. The cars screeched up in fine style, halting in the shadow of the warehouse. The whole operation carried that special sense of urgency you had when CI5 were operating.

The men wore flakjaks and carried weapons.

George Cowley, face grim, gave his orders firmly.

'One man on each side – you – you – across the street. Keep a bead on that roof. You two get to the top of the building there. Report in. You and you – ' he went on, detailing a ring of men and weapons about the factory and the man with a gun on the roof.

Bodie looked across as Murphy, shrugging on his flakjak, wandered over. Murphy was a CI5 man with a lean raw face, and hard eyes, extremely muscular in a lithe, sinuous way.

'What's happening?' Murphy demanded.

Bodie said: 'Madman on the roof . . .'

He glanced up.

Up there Stacey wangled their little invention out over the parapet. The mirror taped to the stick gave him a reasonable view of the street directly below. He'd quite enjoyed it when Barker had sprayed the butcher shop with bullets. Now he could see the men down there, clustered together and talking, and the cars bringing more.

'Activity down there,' he said, swivelling the mirror.

Barker made no bones about it, and as Stacey turned to look at him, said: 'Ginger it up.'

Barker tossed one of their grenades to Stacey.

Stacey's teeth showed as he caught the grenade.

He pulled the pin and lobbed the grenade off into space. The clip sprang free. The grenade hurtled down.

Down there Murphy was saying: 'What's he got up there?'

And Bodie, glancing up, was saying: 'Machine gun and –'

Bodie saw the small black blob arcing out over their heads.

He knew what it was.

He'd seen enough of the things before, had thrown enough in his time and, too true! had had enough chucked at him. . . .

'Grenade!'

He fairly hurled himself at Cowley, took the chief around the waist, hustled him to the deck.

The Mills bomb exploded a few feet above the ground.

Fragments splintered down. Bodie shook his head and, being wise in the ways of combat, took another look up.

21

'Comes another.'

Everyone tried to dig his own private foxhole. The bomb hit the ground and blew. This time a CI5 man was hit.

Cowley struggled up.

Bodie and Doyle leaped up and raced for Charlie Duncombe, who'd taken a bit of splinter in his leg and was saying the most unkind things about the nut case on the roof.

'Back,' shouted Cowley. 'Back.'

The partners helped Charlie hobble off and everyone else scurried away from the hot spot to find shelter around the corner.

In the safety of this area no one was surprised to find Inspector Newton had set up his Headquarters.

Newton was busily chattering into a handset, organising, uniformed officers were busy.

Cowley plunked the street map down and the partners with Murphy gathered around. Sergeant Wood, big and craggy, looked on.

Cowley's polished fingernail stabbed the map with some vindictiveness, testament of the baffled fury he felt.

'Here's the building.' The forefinger jabbed. 'We're here. Over here, empty factory. Derelict buildings.' Now the forefinger almost went clear through the map paper.

'And here's the hospital. He's after the Female Ward, Post-op Intensive Care. Got 'em clearly in his sights. He's already taken the windows out, shot the place up.'

Cowley looked up, the lines on his face drawn.

'Nobody hurt yet. But . . .'

The gathered men didn't like the sound of this.

'Nobody can get to those patients either. Doctor Ramsey tried and nearly got his head blown off.' Cowley jabbed the map again. 'There are six women in that ward. All of them needing constant attention. And no one can get near them.'

No one offered to comment.

Cowley said: 'He's got us. Got us by the short and curlies.'

Inspector Newton came across to report.

'We've sealed off the area. But the media's got hold of it.'

One person in the city took notice of one particular radio broadcast. As the announcer's voice cut in over soporific music, Jack Cobber listened with little interest. As the announcement went on, he cocked his head a little to one side, listening hard.

The announcer's words were: 'We interrupt this programme for a news flash. Early this morning a gunman took over the roof of a Thames-side warehouse. It is reported that shots have been fired at a nearby hospital. But, so far, we have no reports of any casualties. Men from CI5 have already been rushed to the scene. We will be bringing you a fuller report later – '

And the eternal music started up again.

As the CI5 operatives climbed to the roofs of the buildings assigned to them, a picture began to form that George Cowley did not like at all.

Under the open sky, a CI5 man edged to the lip of the parapet. He had a rifle with him, and binoculars, and an R/T. He took a good look at the target building. He could just see, looking up, the row of sandbags.

He put the handset to his mouth.

'Budderton to Cowley.'

Cowley was still studying the map when Bud's call came in.

'Come in,' said Cowley, following the drill.

'I'm as high as I can go. And I'm not high enough.'

Cowley humphed at that. This was beginning to put together the part of the picture he did not much care for.

'Can you see anyone? Any sign of movement?'

'No. I don't have enough elevation. He's still fifteen – twenty feet above me.'

'Stay,' said Cowley in his bulldog voice. 'On watch.'

Cowley traced the outline of the warehouse on the map, his forefinger impatient and yet covering the printed lines with unerring accuracy.

'He's chosen well. That roof ... Nothing higher, nothing overlooks it.' He made up his mind. 'I want to know his strength.'

He turned to Doyle and they began to move away.

'We'll need a chopper.'

Bodie didn't take much notice of that. He was staring away in the opposite direction, looking up into the dazzlement of the sky.

Murphy's gaze followed where Bodie looked.

Up there, thin and black and attenuated against the sky, a slender pencil shape, spearing up, and up –

Bodie said: 'Nothing higher?'

Murphy opened his mouth and then shut it. He could see the chimney, see that it did overtop the warehouse roof. He could also see that the ladder was on this side, and, therefore –

'You're crazy! Go up that ladder, and you're a clear target!'

Bodie smirked a Bodie smirk.

'Who said the ladder? No ... The other side ...'

Murphy, decisively, said: 'You can't do it.'

Bodie nodded. 'You're right.' As Murphy raised his eyebrows at the tough Bodie's quick agreement, that raffishly sleek individual went on sweetly: 'But *we* could.'

Murphy stared owlishly.

Bodie said: 'What did you do during your last leave?'

'I climbed the Eiger. But – but I had guides – and nobody was shooting at me!'

'Come on, Murph. You're the best damned climber on the Squad.' He eyed the chimney. 'A straight brick face. We could hammer our way straight up her –'

Murphy, staring over at the chimney caught the challenge.

'Not straight. Traverse – tie off each section, pin as we go. If that brick's old and something should happen, we've still got a chance –'

He saw Bodie half-smiling at him.

'I couldn't do it alone, Murph.'

24

Murphy returned the smile; but his mobile face remained taut. 'You're crazy.' He moved away and then halted. His shoulders sagged. Then he swung back to face Bodie.

'We're *both* crazy!'

Up on the roof in the cover of the sandbags Barker stared hungrily at the hospital ward.

Stacey did not look nervous, just keyed up.

'Isn't it about time we radioed 'em?'

'Not yet,' Barker told him. 'We still have to play our ace.'

The sound of a distant clip-clopping noise drew his instant attention. He screwed his eyes up against the sky. Far away, a mere flitting dot, a helicopter approached.

Barker smiled his wolfish smile. He banged Stacey on the back, filled with good humour, and yet grim and vindictive with purpose.

'Get to it!'

As Stacey nodded and stood up, he unzipped his coveralls. He wore a woman's dress. One nyloned leg came free of the coverall leg. Barker rummaged out the blonde wig.

From the approaching helicopter a TV link fed the pictures to the ground where Cowley and Doyle watched the monitor.

The voice of the CI5 man in the chopper came down clearly over the radio, and the pictures were reasonable.

'Aerial to Cowley.'

'Come in Aerial.'

'Roof coming up – '

'Don't get too close. Remember, he has a machine gun!'

'Don't worry. We're using the zoom.'

The roof swam in to view. The sandbags piled up, the snout of the GPMG, a raffle of odds and ends. 'There's some kind of makeshift hide down there. Made of sandbags – an old steel door – corrugated iron – there's a lot of debris around. It looks like – it looks like a gun emplacement – '

'Good', said George Cowley, 'God!'

Doyle said: 'He's built a foxhole! A foxhole on the roof!'

The TV screen blurred as the chopper turned. The voice of Aerial came through strongly.

'Something happening on the roof now. A woman is coming out of the hide. She appears to be being forced out into the open. There's someone pushing her out. Her hands are – tied – we're trying to get a better angle. Hostage! The word hostage ... She has the word hostage on a card across her back.'

Now they could see.

White gloved hands pushed the woman out. A rope ran from her neck to the white-gloved hands. The woman was distraught, her blonde hair in a mess.

'A girl!' said Doyle.

The rope jerked. The woman fell down. Now, clearly, the card tied to her back was plainly visible.

HOSTAGE.

Doyle shook his head.

'I was going to suggest we lobbed gas grenades . . .'

Cowley said: 'No good, anyway. The wind would blow the gas away.'

'Just a bomb, then – '

'With a hostage?'

Now the woman was jerked on the end of the rope and stumbled back into the foxhole. She was lost to outside view; but in the cover of the sandbags and the steel roof, Stacey loosened the rope. He was laughing.

'Well, we played our ace!'

'Now,' said Barker in his hard grainy way. 'Let's tell 'em to go away.'

He trained the machine gun up and cut loose with a long burst. Cordite blew, the noise deafened, and both were like the taste of champagne to Roddy Barker.

Cowley immediately called out to the chopper.

'Get out of there, Aerial. That's enough. He's calling the shots.'

'And firing 'em,' said Doyle bitterly.

Aerial said: 'I'm out of range now.'

'No,' ordered Cowley. 'Get out of there. Stand off. Way off. You're making him nervous. And me, too!'

The helicopter turned and the chopping noise dwindled. She bore away until she was once more a mere dragonfly dot against the skyscrape.

Doyle said: 'Who is she? Where the hell did he grab her?'

'I don't know.' Cowley lifted his handset to his lips. 'Cowley to Newton.'

'Come in,' said Newton's voice.

'He's got a hostage on the roof with him. A young girl. Blonde. Don't know who. But we have pictures.'

'What? For Pete's sake, what's he up to?'

Up there in that Foxhole in the Sky Stacey knew what Barker was up to, and wanted to get on with it.

'Phase two?' he said eagerly.

Barker took a Punch and Judy reed and popped it into his mouth. He wiggled it about, got it settled, and spoke.

'Phase two? Not yet – not just yet.'

Barker's voice squeaky and tinny and just like the obstreperous voice of Mr Punch himself. 'Give 'em another half an hour to sweat it out.'

The two CI5 operatives eyed the chimney stack.

It looked big and fat and comfortable at ground level, with solid red bricks and a rotund girth.

But it went on and on, up and up, and as it went up so it became more slender. They tilted their heads back. The stack looked like a thin pencil up there, moving against the sky, ready to topple over on them.

Bodie dumped coils of rope. He'd been lucky to get what he'd specified at such notice. It was nylon, true; but it was blue, instead of the usual yellow.

'One thing about it, Murph. No ice or snow.'

'Feature of the place,' said Murphy in his best travelogue manner.

He wore a nappy harness and the belt was festooned with spring clips and pitons. They were going to use bushels of pitons up this beauty. He wouldn't have an argument.

'I'll go first. Hammer in, clip, go on, bring you up. I'll go on up and – '

Bodie, half chiding, half joking, said: 'Set up a base camp?'

Murphy showed his teeth.

'Yeah.'

He eyed the chimney again. 'You're a better shot than me, Bodie.'

Bodie hefted his rifle.

'I'm the Class A marksman of the whole Squad. Only Doyle gets within a whisker of me. Anyway, he's a handgun man.'

'Yeah. You're modest, too. We may only have the chance of one shot.'

'Should be enough.' Bodie hitched the rifle, jangled the equipment dangling from his belt. 'Let's go!'

Murphy walked up to the stack, selected his spot, hammered in the first piton. He slapped the Krab through the hole. They'd argued amicably about how you spelled Carabiner, or Karrabina, or any combination of K's and C's and R's and A's or ER's. They called the spring clips Krabs. Now Murphy screwed the first one up tight. The blue rope ran through easily.

He put his foot on the first piton, reached up, and hammered in the next. He put them in in a stepped pattern, going not quite straight up, as he'd suggested, but deviating far too little to make a traverse. If they traversed around the stack the maniac on the roof over the way would see them in silhouette and shoot them off like flies on a wall.

Murphy reached up in generous but not stupidly large extensions. Each piton was hammered in firmly, tested, making sure it wouldn't give. The ropes quivered as they were shaken free. Standing on a pin he hammered in the next, and reached up, and so stood on that one and hammered in the next. He formed a lattice work of pitons up the stack.

Bodie followed.

Alex Armstrong and Iain Whitechurch waited below with fresh supplies of pins and Krabs which Bodie would haul up when they ran out aloft. Silly to try to carry the lot up. The nappy harness held him firmly, strapped around his waist and between his legs. The equipment jiggled as he climbed. And the rifle stayed securely slung over his back.

They began to gain height.

The breeze blew up here, and the brick crumbled, and the ground started to get an awful long way down.

But still they climbed up, two little flies crawling up the window pane to eternity.

The helicopter hovered at a distance, turning lazily in the air, clip-clopping towards the warehouse roof and then retreating. Aerial reported they were keeping out of firing range and that the picture on the TV monitor was at maximum on zoom.

On the roof, safeguarded by sandbags, Barker contorted his lips, as much by pleasure at the way his plan was working as fitting in the Punch-sounding voice reed.

'Keeping a discreet distance,' he said. 'Phase two!'

In the Headquarters area out of grenade lobbing range of the maniac on the roof, Cowley and Doyle leaped from Cowley's Rover three and a half and hurried towards Newton.

Cowley carried prints, blow-ups still wet. They showed what the set-up on the roof was like.

'This is the layout.' Cowley gestured. 'He's dug in up there – and that's a paradox if ever I saw one.'

Newton looked savagely at the prints.

'Means to stay, then.'

Doyle said flatly: 'Got a hostage, too.'

The word hostage on the girl's back was very clear.

'I've been through a few of these before.' Cowley took off his heavy glasses and dangled them by an ear piece. 'But never one so organised.'

'Yeah,' said Doyle. 'But what does he want? What's it about?'

The answer to that question came when Sergeant Wood called from a radio car. He held the car mike and was listening to the set.

'Sir! Got something coming in on a dead frequency. Funny. "Man on the roof" asking for "Man in charge".'

Cowley walked across and took the mike.

'This is Cowley.'

The Punch and Judy voice scratched from the receiver. It was odd and unrecognisable.

'And this is the man on the roof. Expect you wonder what I'm doing up here?'

The others walked across to stand listening by Cowley.

The Punch voice went on scratching.

'But, by now, you know just what a position I'm in, don't you? Just in case, I'll spell it out. I'm up here with a very good view, a very good view, of the hospital.'

Through the sights of the machine gun the hospital ward looked as vulnerable as it was. A squirt of bullets and everyone was in danger.

'I've got guns and plenty of ammo. I've got food, too. Enough to last for a month. Not that it's going to take you that long to come to your senses. And, just in case – '

Doyle tensed, expecting a lashing blast of fire; but the Punch voice went on squeaking.

'Just in case you're thinking of busting that door in behind me – if you could bust it in – you've seen the sand bags. But, just in case, I've covered my bets. I've got myself a hostage.'

Cowley said: 'Who is she?'

'Never mind who she is. She's my insurance, that's all.'

'Against what?'

'Against you not meeting my terms.'

'What are they?'

On the roof Roddy Barker felt the triumph welling.

'Simple. A million pounds.'

Chapter Two

The Punch and Judy voice rasped over the radio.

'That's right – a million! Nothing higher than a ten and in two strong suitcases.'

Slowly, speaking with great caution, Cowley said: 'That'll take time to raise.'

'I've got plenty of time. All the time in the world. But – ' And here Barker looked callously through the sights of the machine gun. 'Those patients down there. How much time do *they* have?'

'All right,' snapped Cowley, savagely. 'All right. If we agree, what's the system?'

'Get the money first. Then I'll tell you.'

'Listen – the hostage – '

The scratchy voice broke in demandingly.

'That's all I'm going to say now. Get the money. Then I'll talk some more.'

The line went dead. Cowley still held the mike. His face looked as though he was just being restrained from strangling a man-eating lion. He turned on Newton.

'Call the Home Secretary. The Hospital Board. Get that money here.'

Newton opened his mouth, swallowing, then: 'A million!'

Cowley thrust the hand mike at the policeman.

'Do you have a better idea?'

He stalked off. Ray Doyle followed, shaking his head.

In a series of zig zags, the pitons studded the sheer climb of the stack. Murphy hammered them in, one by one, standing on each in turn to reach the next hammering point. Strung together by blue ropes, Bodie faithfully followed. They were ascending. The breeze blew, the clouds flew across overhead, and the ground was a long

long way down, and damned hard if you hit it.

Cowley took the fresh prints as he reached his car and he and Doyle studied the blow-ups more carefully.

Cowley pushed his glasses on more firmly. He tapped the print.

'We know him!'

Doyle showed surprise at the chief's positive tone.

'Look here,' said Cowley, tapping the photo of the girl hostage and the white gloved hands and the rope. 'Here. He's wearing gloves. And that tricked-up voice. That means we know him. He's on record somewhere.'

'And if we know him, if we knew who we were dealing with – '

' – we'd know better how to deal with him.' Cowley looked up. 'Ideas?'

'We-ell – guns, grenades – '

'The R.A.F. armoury break-in?'

Doyle nodded. 'Starting to put two and two together – '

' – but not making four! You didn't get a single lead on that break-in.'

'I know. But – it's a long shot. That ammo clip the bearded one and his girl found – someone had to pack it, handle it.'

'That's a good thought, Doyle. And it's in your court.'

Whilst the police and CI5 attempted to handle the situation, the television news covered the event with telescopic cameras. Their reports added up more and more to Jack Cobber. A man on a roof with a gun and a girl hostage. Police baffled. Yes, Cobber considered, yes that sounded like Roddy Barker's style.

'The area has been sealed off,' said the commentator. 'Restricted even to our cameras. But we are situated on the north side and with our telephoto lens have a clear view of the warehouse building. The building, on top of which sits a man and a female hostage. A few moments ago we caught a glimpse of some movement on that roof. Just a dark shape, not enough for us to register, and certainly not enough to provide a target for the many CI5 marksmen who have this area staked out.'

Maisie walked in then, calling: 'Jack?'

'Sh –'

'We're supposed to be going out. You're supposed to be ready.'

'Can't go out now – ' He gestured to the screen.

The commentator was saying: 'George Cowley, head of CI5, has so far refused to comment on the situation here. "It is very serious," that is all we were able to get from him. And, judging by the hush that has overtaken this small part of London – it *is* serious.'

Maisie looked petulant. 'Jack – what's it to do with you?'

'It could be,' said Cobber. 'I think – it's Roddy.'

Cowley felt he had to check again with Doctor Ramsey.

The ward looked still a shambles. Patients were moaning. Some had managed to help themselves; but some had not. Nurse Rutley looked all in, shattered by the experience, yet determined to carry on.

Ramsey attracted the attention of a woman moaning in pain. 'Mrs Tembridge – I have some morphine here, painkiller.' He shook the box. 'I am going to toss them to you – can you hear me, Mrs Tembridge?'

She stopped writhing, and with a face bearing the utter stillness of pain, turned to face Doctor Ramsey.

He threw the box of pills. Weakly, Mrs Tembridge reached out, clumsily, and the box fell to the floor.

The Doctor heard Cowley at his back. He turned beseechingly.

'For pity's sake – you must do something!'

'Doing all we can. He'll give us a deadline soon.'

'I'll give you mine now.' Ramsey was swinging his stethoscope to emphasise what he had to say. This was a crisis. 'Unless I can get to those patients within the hour – '

And all George Cowley had to offer was: 'We're doing all we can, Doctor.'

Staring at the patient who was moaning again in terrible dry reachings of pain, Nurse Rutley said: 'It's not enough.'

The words were forced from her by the horror. 'It's not enough.'

She lurched forward, heading for Mrs Tembridge. She moved like a wooden doll – and the ferocious burst of machine gun fire splattered over her head, raking the ward, shattering pieces from the far wall. The noise started the screaming again.

Cowley leaped forward and dragged Nurse Rutley out of range. The firing stopped at once, and Nurse Rutley sagged into Cowley's arms, a limp, sobbing bundle.

Ray Doyle, the ex-copper whose hair did not obey orders all the time, rather like its owner, did two things. He checked with Forensic and the lab turned up a smudged thumb print. Among all the others on the ammoclip – the hippie who had found it, the coppers who'd handled it, a plethora of other smudges – he found a partial thumbprint.

'I wouldn't go into court with it – '

'Who!' demanded Doyle. His voice rang in the Forensic Lab.

'Paul Stacey.'

Doyle snatched the records. He scanned them swiftly.

'GBH. Petty larceny. A small-time hoodlum,' said the Forensics man, Merton, who knew his own job.

'And,' said Doyle. 'Look at his background! Army at seventeen, sergeant armourer. A knowledge of weapons – ' They stared at each. Finally, with meaning, Doyle said: 'Paul Stacey.'

The second thing Doyle did was nip round to see Tessa, who, so information said, was Stacey's current girlfriend. A pretty girl, around twenty-five, with everything a man needed and who was shrewd enough to roll with the punches, Tessa did not welcome Doyle's intrusion. Her flat was smart. She queened it here. At first she denied all knowledge of Stacey; but using all the techniques perfected over dozens of similar interviews, Doyle got nearer to the truth. When he found a spot of gun oil, Tessa caved in.

That and the joint she'd been smoking when Doyle barged in.

'Who's he working with?' demanded Doyle.

She tried to stall; but eventually she told Doyle: 'He phoned somebody a couple of times. I saw him, though. He came to pick Paul up last week. I saw from the window.'

'Car?'

Tessa shook her head. 'Cab.'

'What did he look like?'

'Average. About ordinary. He had dark hair, and a big moustache – '

'Not good enough.'

Doyle waited, seeing his threats working. Then she said, as though suddenly remembering: 'Dunstan. That was his name. T. Dunstan.'

'Now how could you know that?'

'He was carrying a bag thing. Valise. And it was stencilled on the side. Big white letters. T. Dunstan.'

Up on the roof in their foxhole in the sky Barker looked at his wristwatch. He grunted.

'About time we gingered 'em up.'

Stacey and he knew about the grenade launcher. They knew how to operate the weapon. The grenade fitted nicely. Barker aimed the weapon and held it. He slipped the reed into his mouth. He called out on the radio frequency they had selected and now had all to themselves.

'It's your friendly man on the roof again.'

Cowley, called to the radio, tuned to that particular wavelength, listened after acknowledging.

'You can see the top of that empty warehouse to the north?' Barker could imagine all the eyes below swivelling to look. 'Well, keep watching.'

He fired.

Cowley, Newton, Sergeant Wood, all of them, jumped as the big bang crashed across the sky. Smoke billowed up, a miniature mushroom. The crashes persisted, telling of bits and pieces of the ancient building falling down.

36

Up the chimney stack Bodie and Murphy felt the blast. The maniac over there couldn't see them surely? But he'd damn-well shot a damned great grenade at the building, nearly knocked them off. They hung onto the ropes and swung from their pitons.

Murph had hammered well. The pitons held as they swung. Bodie blew out his cheeks and then let out a breath. He just wanted to get to the top and unlimber the trusty rifle and let that maniac over there on the roof have one straight into his damned foxhole.

They took fresh grips on the ropes and pitons, Murphy gestured down, Bodie nodded, grimly, and they started up again.

The blast pleased Roddy Barker no end.

'Plenty more where those came from. And soon I'm going to start using 'em.'

Stacey actively assisted by bringing up another grenade. Barker went on in a gloating voice.

'So that makes two barrels I've got you over. The hospital and every damned building I can see from up here.'

Cowley said, hating the desperation in his voice: 'For God's sake! We've sent for the money. It's on its way.'

'Just make sure it doesn't take too long.'

As Cowley lowered the handset in a helpless little gesture, his R/T bleeped. He flicked it on.

The radio voice said: 'Four five to HQ.'

'Come in, four five.'

'Dunstan,' said Doyle's voice. 'Thomas Henry Dunstan. Ex RAF Flight Lieutenant. Cashiered in '78. Stationed RAF Regiment, Pirbright. Last known address, The Pines, Camberley.' The rush of words made Cowley visualise Doyle's round animated face, the flush along his cheeks, the way his hair would be leaping about. Doyle was onto something. 'I'm on my way!'

The R/T died and the car radio spluttered. The sound of the Punch and Judy voice grated on Cowley's nerves.

'That's long enough. I'm loading another grenade now—'

'No!' Cowley hammered it out. 'No! We're doing all we can. The money's sent for and – ' He heard before he turned and saw. The sound of heavy tyres squishing and then the sight of a low fast armoured car trundling in gave him a tremendous sense of relief. 'No – it's here. The money's here.'

Up on the roof a mirror taped to a stick angled so that Stacey could follow what went on below. The armoured car halted and guards jumped out, to run around and start the procedure for opening the doors. He showed his pleasure as he swung back to Barker.

'That's it. You did it. You damned well did it!'

Barker said in his hard grainy voice: 'Not yet.'

Cowley spoke into the radio handmike.

'We've got the money. Two strong suitcases, like you said. What now?'

For a moment nothing happened. The silence was acute, broken only by the distant – the very distant – sound of the chopper. Then someone yelled and pointed up.

Two ropes snaked down the side of the warehouse. At the ends grappling hooks swung and clanged against the old grimy London Yellow bricks. First one and then the other hook hit the ground. They lay there like elephants' trunks in a drought.

Barker's plan was working. 'One man,' he said with the Punch reed in his mouth. 'Just one man comes out and attaches those cases to the hooks. Make sure they're secure. Make quite sure, because if there's any foul up, I'm still aiming at that ward.'

In the moments that passed with agonised slowness for Nurse Rutley she could hardly bear to hear the moans from her patients. Doctor Ramsey was doing what he could by remote control. But on the ward the picture was one of hopelessness –

'Please – ' called a patient. 'Please.'

'Won't be long now,' said Nurse Rutley, not knowing how long it was going to be. 'Won't be long.' She looked at Doctor Ramsey. 'Please God!'

At the base of the warehouse with the foxhole in the sky on its roof, Cowley finished off attaching the suitcases to the grapnels. He stepped back. Immediately the lines began to tauten. They began to lift. The suitcases soared up alongside the wall, rising higher to the sandbagged emplacement.

Up on the rim of the chimney Murphy paused, hanging out of sight of the warehouse roof. He sounded savage.

'Looks like the payoff. We're too late.'

Bodie sounded by contrast cooler than an un-de-frosted fridge. 'Never too late, Murph.' He started to haul his rifle up around his shoulder. 'Never too late.'

Over on that warehouse roof the suitcases came over the edge and thunked down. Barker licked his lips. The cases were opened, out of sight, and the stacked banknotes were revealed like the Ark of the Covenant to those without faith.

'Twenty-five years,' said Barker, whispering. 'I've waited twenty-five years to see this sight.'

Then he was back to the hard, grey, grainy Roddy Barker. He tossed the blonde wig at Stacey. he slipped the reed into his mouth and called out on the radio.

'Look at the roof.'

Cowley and the others looked up obediently. After a moment a hooded figure appeared with the girl pushed ahead. The duo looked both menacing and heartbreaking. Cowley sucked in his breath. The maniac wasn't going to push her over, was he?

'My hostage,' came the scratchy voice. 'From here on, I'm her shadow. So you do exactly what I say. Exactly, d'you hear!'

'We understand.'

'I want the area cleared. Everyone. You – your men – everyone cleared as far as I can see. Then I want a car. Full tank. I want a car parked by the – '

Barker had it all worked out, knew exactly where he'd get the dumb idiots to bring up their footling car. Then Stacey in the wig and dress gave a yell. Barker whirled.

39

A dark figure showed on the top of the chimney stack. There was the wink of steel and then a flash.

The bullet cracked between Barker and Stacey.

They both hit the deck, and then Barker was lunging for the foxhole, scooping up a machine carbine, snouting it up. His face was congested. His lips writhed. He looked mad, mad clean through utterly bananas, as he aimed the machine carbine and pressed the trigger.

Murphy cursed as his shot missed. He couldn't see anyone, and he aimed for another shot and then a man erupted from between the sandbags. There was a blast of fire. Murphy felt the slugs hitting him, and then he wasn't feeling very much at all. He slid down on his rope, and dangled, his rifle swinging on its strap below him. He swung around as Bodie, frantic, tried to get past.

'Murph! Murph!'

Barker flung the machine carbine down and grabbed the radio mike. He spluttered in his near-incoherent excitement.

'That was a dumb move! And I warned you! Any foul up –'

Cowley broke in strongly. 'No! No – that was outside of my orders. Don't shoot. We're trying to go along. Don't shoot.'

Barker now had his machine carbine back up again, ready to blow the men away who'd climbed up the stack.

'There's another man up there. He's got a rifle.'

The moment hung – if Barker cut loose with his machine carbine then Murphy was a gonner, and Bodie, too, trying to get around the wounded man.

Cowley sucked in a breath. He didn't pretend to be brave; but when a job had to be done it had to be done.

He ran out into the open, a clear target for a gunman on the roof.

'Bodie!' he called. 'Three seven! Get rid of that rifle! Throw it down!'

Bodie was consumed with anger. They'd made a right pig's nest of it. He was trying to get Murph up a bit to ease

40

him, and Cowley's words riding the radio waves over his intercom made him see red.

'He shot Murph!'

'For God's sake! We have a deal going here.'

'And I have a wounded man.' He looked at Murphy. 'Murph . . . Murph!'

Murphy's eyes flickered open.

'I'm okay, Bodie. Shoulder. I'm okay . . .'

'A deal, Bodie!' Cowley was shouting. 'Did you hear that!'

Bodie was tangling himself around in the ropes, halting the swing. If Murph was temporarily all right then Bodie, perforce, must get on with the job in hand.

He started to bring his rifle up into the aiming position. He'd get a shot off, and he'd hit the bastard over there. If he was quick enough he'd get him before the maniac loosed off another burst of machine carbine fire.

Cowley went on yelling, his sandy hair glinting, his face furious.

'Did you hear that, Bodie! Bodie! You're going to foul up the whole thing.' He could feel everything going wrong, just because Bodie was being typically Bodie.

'I am ordering you to throw down the rifle! *Bodie!*'

A long, long moment followed.

Then, sullenly, Bodie unclipped the rifle from the safety cord and let the weapon slip away down the sheer face of the chimney.

Chapter Three

The rifle took a long time falling down the outside of the chimney. Mixed up with Bodie's angry reactions was the thought that there went smash a good weapon. That was waste he didn't like. He looked across at Murphy.

'I can't help much – can't use my arm.'

'Just hold still, Murph.' Bodie had dropped his own weapon; but he looked with fascination at Murphy's rifle, dangling below the wounded man. 'I'm coming for you – '

'No! We'll both go – '

'I'm coming down.'

Bodie had more confidence in Murphy's piton-hammering skill than the mountaineer had himself, it seemed.

On the ground Cowley picked up the fallen and smashed rifle. He, too, spared a fleeting moment for a thought of the waste. Weapons were merely things, objects. As always, it was the finger on the trigger, the eye and brain behind the sights, that mattered. And if you wanted to remove temptation, deprive maniacs like Stacey up above there, of the opportunity of acquiring lethal objects, then he'd agree with that, up to a point. Of course, you'd have to consider banning motor cars as lethal objects as well, and one or two other things, objects, that could be abused. . . .

The Punch voice clattered from the radio as Cowley walked back.

'That's better. Now we'll start again.'

This fellow really had the angles figured out, and Cowley felt a nasty presentiment that he was going to be more difficult to deal with than even the Squad had considered at first. A call came through from the hospital, a desperate, a frantic call, and Cowley radioed up to the gunman on the roof.

'Man on the roof, listen. We just heard from the hospital. Patients there are in a bad way. We have to let a doctor get to them.'

'Soon', came that hateful Punch voice, 'as we're on our way.'

'But we've met your demands. We've – '

'Not yet. Not until I'm home and clear.'

'These are sick people. They never did you any harm.'

'They're part of society, aren't they? Pay their rates and taxes? Sit on juries!' At these vehement words a little dint of puzzlement appeared on Cowley's forehead, then the high-pitched whining voice went on: 'They're your problem. Sooner you get us away, sooner you can get to them.'

Cowley fumed and listened on.

'Here's the deal. A car, full tank like I said, then, I'm coming down the stairs with my hostage. Be a gun in her back the whole time. And I'll be carrying a grenade, pin out, ready. If I see anyone on those stairs, anyone at all . . .'

'There won't be anybody.'

'Better not be. Or there's going to be a big bang.'

'Where's the car taking you to?'

Cowley didn't really expect an answer to that one.

The infuriating voice whined on: 'Tell you about that later. Just get that car here.'

'On', said Cowley, 'its way.'

'That', said the radio-voice, 'is fine. Just fine. Give you final instructions later.'

Doyle reached The Pines and screeched to a halt, slewing the Escort. The front door was locked; but Doyle opened it without a key when the bell produced no response.

He went through the house like a tornado, and then emerged on the front steps, annoyed. He looked about. The spot was nice, reasonable comfort and some privacy. The garage to the side was not locked and he went in and poked around. Oil stains on the floor looked new.

A pile of sacking in one corner looked promising, and he pulled the smelly sacks aside to reveal drums marked with the big letters spelling AVIATION SPIRIT.

Aviation spirit was what kept the Air Force flying.

As he stood there the distant clip-clopping sounds started and died. That was no string of horses clip-clopping along the road. Doyle ran out of the garage.

Now the sounds of a helicopter's engine barroomed up, and they were coming from a spot not a million miles away.

Doyle hared around the back of the house, spotted the white-painted gate in the fence and the paddock beyond.

He vaulted the fence and ran along the edge of the woods, the Pines from which the house took its name.

The wind caught at his unruly hair as he halted on the edge of the woods and stared across the grass at the helicopter.

She'd been painted up with Police markings, and the decals looked new.

At the controls hunched a dark figure; but Doyle was confident he could make out a big moustache.

He took out his revolver, hefted it, and then, crouched over, started off towards the chopper.

Inspector Newton walked across to Cowley with the gait of an enraged and frustrated man of high temper. He looked savage.

'He's won!'

Cowley said: 'Pay-off been made?'

'No. But we're close.' He hesitated. Then: 'Can't we stall him?'

'*This* man? You're joking.'

Newton's resentment almost burst clear through. But he ground out: 'Hopeful. All right. Another five minutes. We'll be ready to do as he says.'

Up on his chimney and now satisfied that Murphy, although wounded, was not going to die, Bodie made sure he was safely hooked on. Then, slowly, without any fuss, he began to draw up the safety cord from which depended Murphy's rifle.

Below that tall finger of brick with the two dangling men a car drove past, turned and approached the indicated parking spot by the block. Hot and resentful eyes watched the car from the shadows as the police and CI5 men remained silent and concealed.

The driver got out and ran like a beetle for cover. Cowley guessed the driver imagined he was going to be shot in the back at every stride he took.

He lifted the handmike.

'Well, there it is. Your carriage awaits.'

Stacey used his mirror to check out the ground below very thoroughly. He nodded to Barker.

Barker said: 'All right. Now, everyone back. I don't want to see a living thing. If I do, it won't be living long. Nor will my hostage.'

The area below cleared of men.

Barker at last, at long last, felt he had pulled it off. The area below was deserted, the car stood silently waiting. The cash was stacked in the suitcases.

He turned to Stacey.

'We've done it!'

Now he took the tiny transmitter, one of the pair Dunstan had fixed, and spoke into the mike.

'Jackpot! Jackpot!'

His voice quivered with excitement, and he could feel the blood thumping in his temples. This was what he'd promised himself all those damned long miserable years – and now it was happening, it was here, it was all going down just as he'd planned!

'Jackpot!' he called out over the little transmitter. 'Come and get us!'

As the words Jackpot echoed in Dunstan's ears he revved the engine and lifted the chopper off the ground out of the paddock behind the woods at The Pines. He would follow instructions. The helicopter with the fake police markings started to chop in towards the city.

The police helicopter that had hovered around the warehouse block, keeping an obbo on the foxhole in the sky, attracted Barker's attention. That wouldn't do.

He frowned.

A silly slip like that could wreck everything. Stacey checked below again. The car still stood there, waiting for them. No obnoxious policemen could be seen. He gave the thumbs up to Barker.

Barker called out to Cowley.

'One thing,' he said, savouring the power he held. 'One thing more. The police chopper. Get rid of it.'

'But –' began Cowley.

Barker sounded very tough.

'We don't make a move until it's gone. Out of sight.'

Considering this request – this demand, a demand backed by muscle – Cowley had to acquiesce. He linked with the police frequency and spoke to the helicopter pilot.

'Cowley to Aerial. Return to base. Acknowledge.'

'Wilco,' replied Aerial. 'Returning to base.'

The vanes glinted in the sunlight, and the helicopter turned, a dragonfly among the clouds, scudded away. The sound lasted for a time, and then died. And the breeze blew.

That breeze blew across Bodie, dangling from the chimney stack. He'd fixed up Murphy as best he could, and he had the injured man's rifle.

He scaled back up to the lip, cautiously, and lay out flat.

He twisted to look down, his sleekness only slightly disturbed by these hazardous goings-on.

'How you doing?'

Murphy looked up. His lean face bore marks of what he was going through; but he hung there in his nappy harness, the ropes taut. The rough bandage Bodie had contrived looked stark and white.

Murphy said: 'What?'

'How you doing?'

46

'Hanging around.'

Bodie's mobile lips wrinkled into what might pass for a smile. Murph was okay.

'Sounds like the payoff – pulling out the chopper . . .'

He turned and wriggled his way cautiously around the rim, not poking his head over, waiting to get a good angle shot. If he fell off now he'd swing like a Grandfather Clock's pendulum, and that maniac over there would spray the whole chimney top with lead.

Bodie was very very careful.

Barker and Stacey watched the police helicopter fly away. Stacey wore a big satisfied smile, and Barker again felt the blood in him, proving he was alive, proving he was still the tops, right up to it, able to pull any stunt he could scheme up . . .

'Few minutes more,' he said. 'Just see that chopper well out of sight. Then we'll be coming down the stairs. You can get back to normal again.'

At that Stacey threw him a sidelong glance of such old-fashioned meaning they both wanted to roar. The suitcases were ready. Each took one and strapped it up over his shoulders. Then Stacey halted.

'Barker – do you think Dunstan – ?'

'He heard.' Barker was supremely confident.

Everything had worked so far, everything was going perfectly. There couldn't be a hitch now. He'd bamboozled them all.

'He heard. Nothing to do but listen for our call, was there? He heard. He'll be here any moment.'

'What do you think?' Suddenly Stacey was apprehensive, at this last minute. 'Our chances . . . ?'

Barker had no doubts, not now.

'Perfect. They're down there expecting us, because we've conned 'em into expecting us. They're waiting to cut us down.' Barker did not have to have a shrewd intelligence to know the CI5 men would have their guns in their fists down there, ringing the car, ready to let loose and hit him and spare the hostage. He knew.

47

'But,' he said, and the mockery echoed in his voice. 'We're going to be long gone.'

He heard the chopping clip-clopping and turned, tensely. A police helicopter bore on towards them through the sky levels. He breathed in, steadily, under control again.

'Long gone,' he said.

They watched the approaching helicopter. Barker and Stacey on that warehouse roof where they'd built a foxhole in the sky, and George Cowley and the CI5 men and policemen surrounding that stark building.

The police markings were plainly visible.

Barker smiled. He reached for the little transmitter the RAF man had fixed. 'Now,' he said. 'If Dunstan's little jammer works . . .'

On the ground Cowley stared at the approaching helicopter with mounting fury. When he saw she was not going to deviate from her course to the warehouse, he called out on the radio.

He was incensed that his orders should be so flagrantly disobeyed.

'What the hell are they doing?' he said, and grabbed up the mike and bellowed. 'Cowley to Aerial. Come in – '

The speaker emitted a sudden caterwauling shrilling heterodyne. A torrent of high-pitched unpleasant noise erupted from the speaker. Cowley struggled to bellow his way through.

'Cowley to Aerial! Come in – come in . . .'

But the little jammer was working, and Cowley was not going to talk to his helicopter, let alone the one that flew in overhead, for some time.

The heavy roaring beat of the helicopter drowned out other sounds. The breeze blew and Bodie watched what was going on from his chimney, and drew Murphy's rifle up. Cowley kept yelling into the mike. The police and CI5 men waited, guns ready.

And, on the warehouse roof, framed by sandbags, Roddy Barker felt the huge bubble of triumph rising and bursting in him.

'Give 'em thirty seconds to find out they've been had,' he said to Stacey.

They stared as the helicopter halted above them. She began to descend slowly.

'Come on! Come on!'

Barker was fairly dancing up and down in impatient excitement. He'd done it. He'd done them in the eye. Now he wanted the getaway to be quick and clean.

At last Cowley heard a faint, wavering, badly distorted voice trying to reach him through the whine of the heterodyne.

'Aerial,' he shouted. 'Come in Aerial.'

A faint, far off-splutter.

'Do you read? Withdraw. Stand off. Stand off!'

The distant voice swelled and faded.

'. . . not ours. Grounded . . . on your instructions. Repeat – we are not . . .' A mishmash of interference, and then, riding in freakishly: 'We are not airborne.'

Cowley glared at the speaker as though it had turned into a king cobra and bitten him.

Then he cocked his head up.

He stared at the hovering helicopter with the police markings.

'We've been had.' His face congested. 'We've been conned!'

He drew his handgun and ran out into the open space. The noise of the helicopter made thinking difficult.

On the warehouse roof the noise bellowed and the bluster blew debris everywhere. The chopper hovered and a rope ladder snaked out, appeared to hang for ever in the sky and suddenly, with a thump, hit the roof. The chopper levelled and the ladder swayed, ready and waiting.

Barker nodded and Stacey, still wearing his girl's outfit, blonde wig, dress, the lot, reached up for the ladder.

Watching this, trying to sort out the picture from his chimney stack perch, Bodie saw the girl reaching for the ladder. The villain had worked it well, sending the girl up. A shot would be tricky . . .

Then Bodie's sharp glance spotted the arms raking up for the rope ladder.

Those forearms were not smooth, they were hard and hairy.

Bodie's reactions were those habitual to him, the reactions of a man who had had to act fast to stay alive.

The rifle slapped into his shoulder, the sights came on and he pressed the trigger.

Stacey felt some awful clouting shock smash through his leg. He yelled and let go. He fell backwards into Barker.

Roddy Barker shouted in anger and pushed viciously as Stacey fell against him. He just shoved and grabbed for the ladder.

Stacey fell.

He made a desperate grab for Barker as that hard man pushed past for the ladder.

'Please – ' gasped Stacey, seeing Barker all distorted. 'Please –'

The ladder felt good in Barker's hands; but that bastard on the chimney stack was shooting, and Stacey was useless. Barker stared up, the cords in his neck like ridged iron.

'Go! *Go!*'

The bewildering blattering of the helicopter's vanes, the swirling sensations, the blustering wind bashing at him, streaming his hair, all these meant nothing beside two over-riding sensations. The feel of the ladder in his fists and the weight of the suitcase. He roared up for Dunstan to lift up and away to freedom.

Stacey clawed up. He made a desperate attempt to grab onto Barker's legs.

Roddy Barker kicked his associate clear with unfeeling contempt.

The helicopter began to rise.

Barker screamed up. 'Go! Go!'

Up lifted the chopper and Cowley and his men, far below, fired ineffectual shots skywards.

Clinging to the end of the ladder, rising up into the sky and freedom, Roddy Barker allowed a tremendous grin of triumph to spread all across that hard grey grainy face.

The world dropped away below.

Down there all the little men were running and shouting and waving their arms at him. Some of them were shooting. That was like shooting little pop guns at an elephant. He was Roddy Barker, and he was riding on top of the world. The suitcase dragged on him marvellously.

He'd beaten them all, beaten the world.

He was the tops.

That remarkable picture of the man clinging to the end of the ladder dangling from the helicopter was faithfully picked up by the TV cameras and flashed onto the waiting millions of television screens in homes throughout the country. This was news as it happened, raw news, in the making.

One of the people who stared at the picture of the dangling man on his ladder knew who that tiny figure was.

Jack Cobber and his wife Maisie stared, fascinated. The drama unfolded. As Roddy Barker lifted up to freedom and success and the idiots of policemen below were left baffled, Cobber tried to fathom out his own feelings.

Roddy had done well – damned well!

Maisie kept blinking her eyes, as though she couldn't believe what she was seeing.

And, at the site, Cowley watched the helicopter hovering above the warehouse. No good shooting a little popgun up there; anyway, even if he ordered a rifleman to take a crack the bullet might bring down the chopper and that would make a very nasty mess all around. He stood, staring up, his eyes half-closed in crinkles of skin, his sandy hair glinting, staring up.

Roddy Barker stared up, too, hard and grainy, staring up at the chopper. Then he glanced down. He looked down past his feet and saw all the little men down there like insects. He gloated. Those little men down there –

The little men were growing in size.

The helicopter was descending.

Barker looked up, screaming out: 'Up! Up!'

But the chopper continued to lower down, dropping lightly down towards Cowley and the ring of armed and waiting men.

The television announcer's voice over that remarkable picture said: 'Now the helicopter is starting to descend. It is getting lower. Cowley and his men are moving out to meet the man on the ladder...'

Maisie gripped onto her husband's arm as they stared at the TV set. Both sensed some new and dramatic turn in events. Roddy Barker, on the ladder, was screaming up and they couldn't hear what he was saying in the blattering roar of the helicopter, not the men on the ground or the helicopter or Bodie and Murphy on their chimney stack.

'What's happening?' demanded Murphy, dangling in his harness, the Krabs fully screwed up, the lines taut, the pitons well-driven in.

Bodie shook his head.

'You'd never believe it.'

The helicopter lowered. Cowley and his men stared up. Barker could see them. He could see the guns. He could see the ground, and the hardness of it.

He'd won. He'd beaten them, fair and square, and, at the last furlong, he'd lost, at the last fence he'd taken a tumble.

No hesitation, no hesitation at all, touched his mind.

Staring up, intuitively easing his way into the mind of the man dangling on the ladder, aware of a little of what might be going on in that hard head, Cowley, too, understood.

'No!' he said, taking a quick involuntary step forward.

But Roddy Barker's decision was made.

The white-gloved hands slackened their grip.

They opened. The fingers slid from the bar of the ladder.

The TV announcer, unlike Cowley, was completely unprepared. His voice gabbled in horrified excitement.

'It's terrible – horrible. The man has fallen. Fallen to the ground...'

George Cowley walked slowly forward. His men

remained a pace or two, discreetly, in the rear. He looked down.

The suitcase had burst open on impact, like Barker. Notes scattered about and some scuttered and blew in the little breeze. Cowley looked up.

The helicopter alighted in the yard with a vast fluttering that scattered the notes – none less than a tenner – around in a storming whirlpool of paper.

Dunstan, at the controls, looked shrunken, and his big moustache drooped.

At his side sat Ray Doyle, calm, unaffected externally by the tragedy. Doyle's gun was not too evident. But Dunstan had never been unaware of that gun from the moment Doyle had shown it to him and told him what to do.

Cowley shook himself out of that mood, and told Inspector Newton to contact the hospital. Their long ordeal was over. Now Doctor Ramsey and Nurse Rutley could get back to caring for their patients.

It was over, for them, and for Roddy Barker.

The TV screen managed a shot of Barker, lying dead on the ground. The ground was hard. Jack Cobber stood up. He felt dreadful, light-headed, sorry and relieved. He needed a drink, for sure.

Maisie followed him. She took his arm and he turned to her, visibly affected by what they had both witnessed. Roddy Barker had been a mate.

Finally, Cobber said: 'Could have been me, Maisie. It could have been me . . .'

When the fuss died down, Cowley took Bodie and Doyle up onto the roof of that particular warehouse.

The area appeared bleak. It was silent now, deserted, waiting for the removal of the sandbags and the steel door and the corrugated iron. The G.P.M.G. and the machine carbines would be taken away with very great care.

The three CI5 men stared. They had shared, each in his own way, that experience. But what they were looking at now affected each one differently. This was a foxhole, a foxhole in the sky, and it just was something out of the ordinary to one or the other, something to be smashed to the others, something from the past . . .

Cowley shook his head, summing up, finishing it all.

'I never thought ever to see one of these again . . . Certainly not within the City of London!'

Chapter Four

Bob Willows stood a few paces away from the headmaster of the public school and Colonel Ojuka as the boys swirled around them in the lobby, going from classrooms out to the playing fields. Willows had grown accustomed to this position, half in the shadows. He watched other people, watched what went on, and his hand was never very far from the gunbutt of the Smith and Wesson in his hip pocket.

When he'd retired from the Military Police and they'd taken away his Service sidearm and issued him with this dinky little Smith and Wesson, Gladys had said she didn't know if she should be glad he didn't have such a big gun, or worried because he now had such a small one. Either way, Bob Willows could use the revolver, and would, too, if any idiots cut up rough with the people the department put in his care.

This Colonel Hakim Ojuka, for example. Now there was a fine figure of a man, tall and commanding, black as the Ace of Spades, a man who commanded instant respect by sheer force of personality. Mind you, there'd been trouble in his country of Betan, and he'd been, if not kicked out, then told to take a rapid leave of absence. Bob Willows had been given the job of looking after Hakim Ojuka and his wife Kutunda, his fourth wife, Willows thought, not quite sure.

If Ojuka was a fine figure of a man, Kutunda was a remarkable woman. She was beautiful in any man's language, seductive, calm, self-possessed, graceful – and by the way she was taking no interest at all in why she and her husband had come to the public school today, Willows saw that Ojuka's son by his first wife felt more lonely than he ought to.

Felix, dressed in school clothes, polished and scrubbed, stood quietly with the head and his father and his father's new wife. They talked about him over his head. Willows saw all that. Willows's own son, whom he and Gladys adored, had wanted nothing to do with the military life that was all his father had known. So Willows stood there, in the shadows, watching the party, aware of the rush of schoolboys past his legs, his hand near his hip pocket, and he watched.

The head master in his best patrician way, was saying: 'Well now, Felix. I think we've shown your father the nuts and bolts of the school, don't you? If we've missed anything, you can tell him about it in your letters. I'm sure you'll have lots of things to write about, once you're under way.'

Colonel Ojuka smiled at his son.

'Promise me that you will do that, my son. This is a fine school, and I want to hear that you are doing well, so that I can be proud of you. So that Mister Harper here can be proud of you.'

'Yes', said Felix, quietly, 'Father. I will try.'

His gaze flickered to Kutunda; but there was nothing there for him. Harper, the head, sensed something of this and pushed it smoothly along.

'Good, that's the spirit. Now if you cut along to Four B, you can join your class with Mister Seaborn. I'll be talking to you all later, in the refectory.'

Ojuka extended his hand to his son. Solemnly, Felix shook hands with his father. They were much alike, and one day Felix would be as tall and handsome and rugged as his father.

'Goodbye, Felix. And I will come again, soon. That I promise you.'

'Goodbye, father.'

The boy's head was set more than he realised at an upright, arrogant angle, and Ojuka nodded, satisfied. They watched Felix until he had gone, then the head ushered the party outside where other parents moved about and boys attempted to behave themselves.

'All in all, I don't think there's much cause for concern, Colonel,' he said. 'Apart from an initial shyness, I'd say your son was settling in with us very well.'

'That pleases me, Mister Harper, there is nothing in this world as valuable as knowledge. And I feel sure you will educate him well here.'

'Well, we'll do our best for him. I'm glad you were able to come and talk to us today. I must say, I hadn't expected the pleasure, under the – er – circumstances.'

Willows saw that the head was skirting difficult waters here, trying to be tactful.

Ojuka smiled. 'It was not easy.' He glanced at Bob Willows, a shadow in the background. 'As you can see, your Government is very protective toward me at this moment. And so I must not linger.' He shook hands with the head. 'Goodbye, Mister Harper. We shall, of course, meet again.'

'Yes, of course.' The head's look took in Bob Willows and what his presence implied. 'Goodbye, Colonel. Madame.'

They walked away as the head turned his attention to other waiting parents. After all, Colonel Hakim Ojuka was something of a celebrity, and perhaps particularly because of his own troubled position. Bob Willows let them walk ahead, as was right and proper, but he kept a little to one side as they went towards the car park, and his restless gaze probed everywhere. He might not be privy to all the secrets of his masters; but the Major had detailed him for this duty with the stern injunction to keep his eyes open. Bob Willows did just that as Colonel and Madame Ojuka walked towards their parked car.

A car nosed out of the line and turned down towards them. Nothing special in the car; Willows saw it tooling along, mentally filed it away. Just a black Vauxhall with a nice polish.

The cars gleamed in the sunshine. The sound of schoolboys racketed on the air. Willows felt – something, a sense of impending action he could never identify. But it was a sense that had put him where he was now.

He snapped his attention back to the black Vauxhall.

When it happened, it happened fast.

His hand was raking back to his hip for the new Smith and Wesson 38 when the rear doors of the car opened and two men leaped out.

Gunfire blasted that cool public school atmosphere.

Hit immediately, Bob Willows fell.

He hit the ground hard, feeling the numbing shock of slugs in him; but the revolver snouted and he fired. He hit the nearest gunman, flung him back against the car.

A red haze clouded Willows's vision.

He had a quick glimpse of the Colonel whipping out a silver automatic and of blasting the second man. The big bullets cut the would-be assassin down in his tracks. The man against the car levered up, his gun still pointed.

Willows squeezed the trigger again.

The retired military policeman and the murderer shot each other, exchanging mutual bloody death.

Willows sprawled forward. He still gripped the little Smith and Wesson.

Ojuka spared his bodyguard a single glance. He looked at Kutunda. She stood, immobile amidst the carnage, her hands to her face. There was something withdrawn and primeval in the way she stood there, unmoving, as bullets snapped about her.

The driver, seeing his two comrades cut down, swore and revved the engine. He gunned the car away, attempting to reach the end of the car park and the tree-lined road.

Colonel Hakim Ojuka lifted his silver-coloured automatic. He took careful aim. When he pumped bullet after bullet into the fleeing car his face registered a pleased excitement, a genuine appreciation of the situation.

The car slewed abruptly. It reared over as its offside wheels hit the grassy bank. Headlong, with a dead driver at the wheel, it careered on and smashed full into a solid oak tree trunk.

Instants later the car mushroomed into a bloating ball of fire. The concussion strewed itself and the car across the car park. Ojuka stood, calmly contemplating the results of his shooting. A tall column of black smoke gushed, humping and coiling, from the wreck.

Then, coolly, he let the automatic drop down to his side from the aim. He turned. His bodyguard, the dead assassin, lay crumpled. He walked towards his wife, and Kutunda slowly came back to life.

But life would never return for Bob Willows.

CI5 HQ took in the call and directed two of their agents to head for the scene.

Doyle took the R/T call and Bodie, at the wheel, screeched the silver-grey Capri into a complete circle and burned rubber belting out towards the public school. Doyle was thrown back against the upholstery. He glanced across at his partner.

Bodie's lip curled.

'A shoot-out? Outside a public school? I don't know what the upper class is coming to.'

'Hard to get places, these days,' commented Ray Doyle, playing it along with his partner. 'Perhaps you've got to blast your way in.'

'I take it you were never privileged enough – '

'Oh, yeah? Why'd you take it?'

Bodie spared a quick glance for Doyle.

'You never wear a tie – dead giveaway –'

'Is it?' said Doyle. 'What was yours, then? Eton? Winchester?'

'That's not a school . . . That's a rifle.'

Doyle raised his eyes heavenward.

'Yeah. That's what I thought. Dead giveaway.'

Bodie whirled the Capri around the next roundabout, giving two old ladies in a Datsun a heart-attack and the car a severe case of wheel-wobble, and hared along the open road.

Doyle said: 'What about this African?'

'Ojuka. Not much. Fled his native land just before the coup there, about a month ago. I didn't know we had him.'

'Somebody,' said Doyle, and the grimness in his words pointed up the reason for all the banter. 'Somebody did.'

The scene in the carpark of the public school still smoked raw with the tangible air of the aftermath of violent death. The police, both uniformed and plain clothes, were there, and the ambulances; and the school teachers were doing their best to shepherd parents and school boys away.

George Cowley's Rover three and a half was there.

George Cowley was there. The chief of CI5 was in an ugly mood.

The thickset, upright man in civilian clothes of a tweedy cut, standing by a staff car, was quite clearly an army officer in mufti. He looked not so much upset as wearily indignant at Cowley's annoyance.

'It's no good sounding off at me on this one, Cowley,' said Major Danby. 'I merely obeyed the request from the Home Office.'

'Then,' said Cowley, his head going up, 'tell me why they should make such a request to you, Major. Or to military security at all?'

'Because Colonel Ojuka wanted to be here today. And Colonel Ojuka is a very persuasive man, as I've no doubt you'll discover.'

'Which means you've been relieved of the responsibility, and the buck's been passed to me.'

Major Danby spoke coldly. 'If you want to put it like that . . . .Yes. I lost a good man just now, Cowley, and I wouldn't say I was relieved about that.'

'You're well aware that's not what I meant.' Cowley felt true sympathy for the Major, a man who had lost another man in line of duty. That was one of the burdens they shared. 'What riles me is how it happened in the first place. Ojuka's not exactly a guest of the military in this country –'

'Agreed.'

The ambulancemen were finishing up. Bob Willows,

retired military policeman, slid away into the ambulance, and Major Danby felt the chill of that.

'If you're interested,' he told the chief of CI5, 'I'm also agreed that your department should have been in from the beginning. This is a strong-arm diplomatic matter as much as anything else.'

A Capri drove into the carpark. Major Danby watched. Then he said: 'And there's your muscle, unless I'm mistaken.'

Bodie and Doyle alighted from the car, took swift looks around, spotted their boss, and headed for Cowley. By the way they walked Danby could tell.

'I'll leave you to give them your words of wisdom, Cowley. I've some explaining of my own to do elsewhere this afternoon.' He moved towards his staff car. 'Give my regards to the Colonel and his lady, won't you?' Although Danby spoke drily, he was feeling savagely at odds with the world. 'I hope they haven't been too upset . . .'

As Major Danby settled in his staff car, Cowley walked across. He leaned on the sill. He looked concerned.

'He killed two of them himself, you say?'

'Apparently so. He's no stranger to a dangerous life. And he obviously goes armed.' He cocked an eye at Bodie and Doyle as they walked up. 'So he should be in good company.'

'Who's the woman? His mistress?'

'No, his wife – or, at least, one of them. He has four. This one is the most recent and the most favoured.' Danby put a forefinger to his clipped moustache. 'So he brought her with him when he skipped. She's addressed as Madame Ojuka, by the way.'

'No doubt,' said Cowley in his driest way, 'they all are. I'll keep in touch, Major.'

'I'm sure you will, Cowley.'

Danby nodded, the driver saw the signal in the mirror, and the staff car pulled away.

Cowley turned to regard his two agents – his two so-called ace-agents. People called Bodie and Doyle the Bisto

Kids. They were tough, competent, knew their business, and stood no nonsense. They were also human. This one might come as a pleasant surprise.

Doyle was looking after the staff car bearing Major Danby away.

'What,' said Doyle, 'is the Fourteenth Heavy Metal Brigade doing here? It's not war, is it?'

Cowley turned with such savagery on Doyle, he caught it in time, caught himself, and was able to make his remark the usual jaw-champing no-nonsense ticking-off habitual between them.

'It's never anything else, Doyle.' He gestured to the scene. 'Or would you call this peaceful?'

'No sir.' Doyle's face expressed complete resentment of authority; but as they watched the ambulance and saw the pools of blood, still smelled the stink of the blown-up car on the air, he had to agree. 'I wouldn't.'

'I'm glad to hear it, because you two are going to be standing where he stood.' They could see into the ambulance, where the bullet-riddled body of Bob Willows waited to be carted away. 'Right where he stood, right next to Colonel Ojuka.' He let that sink in, did Cowley, let them absorb what he was saying. 'So, if you'll follow me, I'll make the introductions.'

Before they followed their chief, Bodie and Doyle looked again at the ambulance. In there a man who was by way of being in the same trade as themselves lay wrapped in his own blood. They exchanged sombre looks. Well, what the hell; they were all paid for this job, weren't they? Bodie strode out, head up, chin in, breathing deeply.

Doyle walked along with his hair unruly in the breeze, meditating the unkind cuts of fate.

Bodie said in his casual yet abrupt way: 'This Ojuka. Is he a friend of ours?'

Cowley half-turned, still walking on.

'Politically, yes. Diplomatically, he's more of a thorn in the flesh than anything else.'

Doyle had to say: 'And we're going to be the Elastoplast.'

Cowley favoured Doyle with a cutting look.

'CI5 has been instructed to safeguard the Colonel, if that's what your juvenile metaphor was meant to convey, Doyle.'

Doyle remained perfectly unabashed.

'Something like that, sir. What's he doing here? Apart from getting his kids educated?'

'He wants to re-establish himself in power, and he needs our help to do it. Just how much we'll give him is to be decided at a conference this week. He was supposed to stay under wraps until then.' Cowley half-glanced back at the scene they were leaving. 'This is what happened when he didn't.'

'If he's trouble, why are we playing ball with him in the first place?' Bodie wanted to know. 'I thought we'd done our bit over there.'

'Because the military coup that replaced him isn't looking Westward for its ideology. The game hasn't even started in Africa yet, Bodie.'

'Which way,' said Doyle, 'does Ojuka look?'

'Heavenward,' said Cowley, walking briskly on. 'So they tell me.'

Bodie and Doyle stared after the erect form of their chief, and then at the scene of the massacre.

'Seems to work,' said Bodie. 'After a fashion.'

'Yeah,' said Doyle. 'Maybe he's got something.'

Inside the lobby the three blinked their eyes for a moment to adjust, and a doctor walked quietly out from the end corridor. His face was calm, not perturbed, and Cowley, for one, felt relief at that.

'Doctor,' he said. 'How are they?'

'They're okay. I've given the lady a mild sedative. Her pulse was a little jumpy.'

'Understandable, having stood in the middle of a gunfight. What about the Colonel?'

The doctor made a little movement of his free hand. 'Unharmed. And steady as a rock. I get the feeling he rather enjoyed the affair.'

Cowley did not look impressed.

'I hope nobody tells that to Major Danby. He's on his way to tell a woman she's just been made a widow out of this.'

The doctor nodded with a quick and understanding sympathy; he saw death as a part and parcel of his daily life: he did not often see death in the guise of a bullet-riddled corpse.

Cowley said, briskly: 'Can we go in?'

'Yes, of course. I'll have a copy of my report sent to you.'

Followed by Bodie and Doyle, Cowley moved down the end corridor and opened the door of the room the head had given over to Ujuka and Kutunda to recover. The study was small, book-lined, brown leather and brown oak, smelling of books and polish. There were two easy chairs, and Kutunda sat in one, not so much slumped as resting gracefully.

For his part, Colonel Ojuka was busily perusing the stuffed bookshelves, flicking through the freight of knowledge and learning, absorbed. He looked across as the three CI5 men entered. Kutunda looked up, and returned the quick appraising glances of the newcomers with a cool direct gaze. Bodie and Doyle looked at her, realised she was a woman, and then concentrated on the dialogue between Cowley and the lady's husband.

'My minister has instructed me to assume responsibility for your continued safety in this country, Colonel. And that of Madame Ojuka, of course. To that end I've assigned these two men to replace the bodyguard who was killed here today.'

Ojuka looked carefully at Bodie and Doyle, and they could see quite clearly he was pondering on them, on their abilities, their courage, their willingness to get killed to protect him.

'The other was a good man,' said the Colonel. 'He died well. Will they do as much?'

Cowley held himself in check and replied diplomatically,

his voice rich and plummy. 'I trust it won't come to that, sir. In all probability, the attack on you today was unco-ordinated. Whoever it was, gambled on your presence here to see your son. We won't offer them that sort of chance again.'

Ojuka smiled at Cowley's positive tone.

'I see,' he said. 'You are the Prophet's man, Mister Cowley.'

Bodie and Doyle glanced one at the other, and Cowley, relaxed now, looked quizzically puzzled.

'How is that, sir?'

'Mohammed says: "Trust in God; but tie your camel first." I take it you would not have allowed me here today.'

Cowley forbore to mention the old saying: 'Trust in God and keep your powder dry.' Instead he agreed vigorously with Ojuka's assumption.

'No, sir, I would not.'

Kutunda interrupted then, and her voice, both Bodie and Doyle noticed, was very easy on the ear.

'Then you are the Prophet's man.'

Ojuka turned to his wife, approvingly, and for a moment the three Englishmen were out of it. Bodie and Doyle rode along with the situation, taking everything as it came, and Cowley simply continued with that bland, half-official, half-mocking smile on his face. Then he said: 'Well, I learn something every day, don't I?'

'As we should, Mister Cowley,' said Ojuka, turning back, gravely, really meaning it. 'As we should.'

Cowley, had he not been George Cowley and very long in the tooth, might have been nonplussed. His smile remained, as he pulled the whole conversation back his way.

'I understand you defended yourself very effectively today, Colonel.'

Ojuka nodded. 'Indeed. It is a habit of mine.'

'A commendable one – although I'm not sure that the minister was aware that his guest carried arms in public. May I see the gun you carry, please?'

For a brief moment, Bodie, for one, thought that Ojuka would refuse. Then, in a studied way, the Colonel opened his coat and took out the silvered auto from the shoulder holster. Cowley handled the weapon with familiarity, and, as always, with the respect for its deadliness any weapon deserves.

Bodie saw the auto and his face tightened, and a gleam of avarice appeared in his eyes. Doyle, the pistol shot on the team, simply stared, his mouth rounding to an O.

'SIG P210,' said Cowley, with deep relish. 'The fancy silvering is not to my taste, Colonel; but the weapon is. One of the finest handguns ever made.'

Ojuka nodded, again, as though indifferent.

'The Schweizerische Industrie Gesellschaft weapon is, indeed, a fine one. But you still have to shoot straight.'

'Agreed.' Cowley handed the superb auto pistol to Bodie. 'Make sure this is kept safely for Colonel Ojuka, Bodie. I'm sure he wouldn't like it to go astray.'

Bodie took the weapon as though taking the Holy Grail. Well, almost . . . He was a long-arm man, himself. He saw Kutunda conceal a small secret smile as he switched his gaze from the silvered auto. 'Yes, sir,' he said, obediently.

Ojuka's eyebrows drew down.

'Mister Cowley –'

Cowley kept a straight bat. 'Yes, sir?'

'The weapon belongs to *me*.'

'Yes, of course,' said Cowley, very smoothly, like greased paper over butter. 'But it's not the policy of CI5 to arm our visitors for their own protection. That's what these men are for. And, I assure you, they're very good at it. So – I think we'll leave it there.' He spoke directly to the partners. 'The Colonel has one of our unlisted accommodations. You'll take him there, and provide security until further orders. Understood?'

Together, they said: 'Yes, sir.'

'I'll be in touch when we have the conference details, Colonel. Good day, Madame.'

When Cowley had gone, Colonel Ojuka remained for a

moment, unmoving. Then he half-turned and said: 'A strong-willed man, this Cowley. Is he always so?'

It had to be Bodie to say: 'Yes, indeed, Colonel. Quite disarming, at times.'

They would take Bodie's Capri.

The partners, assigned a bodyguard job, could feel the way the situation was already working on them. The old adrenalin was flowing. They looked everywhere as they walked towards the car park, looked everywhere without appearing to do so. That was automatic, a part of the job and of themselves.

If anything happened, the adrenalin was on tap, ready to be used. If nothing happened, they'd just be dog-tired at the end of the day.

Then they faced the night.

Doyle felt they ought to make some attempt to establish themselves as people and not merely walking carriers of guns. Bodie couldn't have cared less. Their actions made them people; and this was true.

'Do you have any idea who your attackers might have been, Colonel?'

'Enemies, Mister Doyle. Not enemies of the blood; but men paid to act as enemies.'

'You mean,' said Bodie, 'hired assassins?'

'No. I think not assassins. Had they meant to kill me they could probably have done so without risking themselves so much.'

'Then who?'

Kutunda, quietly, said: 'Not assassins.'

Doyle spoke to the woman in an easy and yet simple way, respect evident but not slavish.

'Did you recognise them, Madame Ojuka?'

She shook her head. The movement was filled with light and grace.

'In the Muslim world, an assassin is a killer, deranged by the eating of hashish; that is how the word was made. Such a practice is not legal here.'

67

At this, Ojuka laughed richly.

Doyle went on: 'Neither is murder, Madame Ojuka. And your bodyguard was shot dead over there. Very dead –'

'As were his killers,' put in Ojuka, hard. 'A swift justice for them, and a fitting one.'

The drive was an affair of short conversations and intervening longueurs. Kutunda was still quiet after the sedative, and Ojuka had much to mull over. The apartment in the mansion block, although luxurious, was not obtrusive. Going up, the partners felt they had to quip about all this to relieve the heavy air of tension they did not want.

'So this,' began Doyle, 'is one of our unlisted accommodations. I wonder how you get on the list.'

'Easy,' said Bodie. 'You phone up Cowley, persuade him you're a vital figure in global strategy, then ask for the keys. He sends them round in a cab –'

Regretfully, Doyle shook his head.

'Wouldn't work.'

'Why not?'

'He', said Doyle with irrefutable logic, 'would recognise my voice.'

Bodie saw the flaw in his pyramidal scheme, and accepted it philosophically.

They went up and into the apartment after the Ojukas.

George Cowley spent a deal of time in the CI5 Headquarters Computer Room. More time than he cared for, liking to be out in the field. But he recognised that in this ultra-modern world, rapid communications, updates and the retrieval of information could take place here, where he might be legging it out in the field for days on end. It was all a part of the changing pattern. And, incidentally, a symptom of the way Cowley had built CI5 into a crime-fighting force.

Major Danby came in, looking rough, and Cowley knew what that was all about.

'Well,' said Danby, puffing out his cheeks. 'That's one meeting I could have done without today.'

'You've seen his wife?'

'His widow, you mean.'

'Yes. How did she take it?'

Danby said it baldly, for their knowledge would not countenance frills here. 'Badly.' He made that irritable gesture with its freight of hidden meaning. 'You hope they're going to be prepared for it in some way. With a husband on active service. But they never are.'

Cowley's sympathy was lively and evident.

'I think we all tend to see each other as immortal, even in this kind of job. Until it happens.'

'Gladys Willows thought that of her husband. What Bob Willows thought – well – '

Cowley brisked onto fresh fields, not caring for the trend of the conversation.

'Our Colonel Ojuka apparently views himself in the indestructible way, from what I've seen of him.'

'Oh, yes. A man of destiny.'

'I've been looking at Betan on the map. Twice the size of Great Britain, and still lost in the middle of nowhere. One great chunk of emptiness. Population practically nil, and barely a mile of road or railway in any of it.'

'No. But you could point some lovely missiles in our direction, if the new junta was disposed to let you do it. At least, all Ojuka wants is for his country to be left alone.'

'With', observed Cowley, 'him at the wheel.'

'Let the diplomats wrangle over it, Cowley. That's their job. Yours is to get him to them in one piece.'

This made Cowley ruminate for a space, reflecting on the wheels of bureaucracy and the use thereof to CI5.

'Was there a *written* request?' he said. 'For Ojuka's little outing today?'

'Yes, there was. Why do you ask?'

Cowley's reaction to the question by asking another was perfectly automatic.

'Do you know who signed it?'

'One of the gnomes, I expect. Somebody's assistant-secretary. I can check it for you, if you like.'

'Yes, if you would, Major.'

Danby touched his moustache. 'What's on your mind?'

'I'm not sure yet. But with two men next to him, I think I should keep my eyes open, where Colonel Ojuka's concerned.'

Ray Doyle had ventured to remove his jacket.

He sat straddling a chair in the lobby of the apartment, next to the table where he'd pushed magazines aside to make room for his R/T intercom. He glanced through the magazines, but his mind was on the job.

Taking his coat off he revealed the shoulder holster and the butt of the handweapon. This, Doyle felt, did not obtrude on this household as it would on a more normal establishment.

This Colonel Hakim Ojuka was some character.

Of course, when he came up against George Cowley, the inevitable had occurred; but, all the same, the Colonel was quite clearly a useful gunhand.

Now his wife, the graceful Madame Kutunda Ojuka, came through into the lobby from the lounge beyond. She carried a cup of coffee. The steam coiled.

'I thought you might like some coffee . . . '

'Thank you,' said Doyle, taking the cup. He did not make a rigmarole out of accepting the coffee.

'Where is your companion?'

The idea of Bodie being called Doyle's companion amused the ex-policeman. He smiled easily.

'He's keeping an eye on things outside. We'll change over soon.' He looked at the coffee. 'I'm sure he could do with a cup as well.' Doyle let a couple of heartbeats pass, then: 'Where's the Colonel?'

'He is reading.' Kutunda's voice, pleasant and light, remained flat and impassive in tone. 'He says if a man is not acting, he should be gathering information. If neither of those, he should be sleeping. He is not a man who likes to waste his time in this world.'

'I can believe that.' Doyle sipped the coffee. 'You been together long?'

'No, not long.' There was, considered Doyle, the suggestion of a veil cast over this woman's words, as though she spoke either by rote, or without full revelation of what she was thinking. Well, everyone did that, if they weren't complete idiots.

'I was brought from a village in the north of Betan, a year ago. I have been with him since then. When the revolution came, he took me with him.' She was thinking back to those times. 'It was a hard journey. But I am young. And Hakim is a strong man.'

The story interested Doyle; but some of the phraseology caught his attention.

'You say you were – brought to him. What does that mean?'

'Very little, in Betan. It means I was chosen for him, that is all. What seems strange to you here is no more than custom, in our country. I was happy to go with him, and to stay with him, when he brought me here. I am his wife, Mister Doyle, that is all that it means.'

Ray Doyle's policeman's nose twitched. There was more here than was being said; but customs were customs, and sometimes if you forgot that you ended up three inches high, with a shrivelled head into the bargain.

Kutunda finished: 'Tell your companion that there is coffee, if he wishes.'

'I'll do that,' said Doyle. 'Goodnight.'

He stared as she went back into the lounge, her gliding walk in the embroidered kaftan very pleasant to see, then his R/T cheeped and he was back to the daily grind.

'Four five,' he said.

Bodie's voice said: 'All quiet on the Western Front?'

'Yeh. The Colonel's in bed, gathering information.'

In his Capri, parked outside the apartment block, Bodie sighed wistfully.

'So would I be, if I wasn't here. I had the lovely Louise

71

lined up for tonight. Fresh off Concorde.' Bodie's mobile lips puckered in remembrance and baffled lust. 'Amazing what that does for her.'

'No,' said Doyle. 'No, you priapismic monster. I meant he's reading.'

The little silence followed, and amused Doyle; then he said briskly: 'We'll turn around in thirty minutes, okay?'

Bodie said: 'Okay. Out.'

He switched off his R/T and sat back, then bent his head, frowning at the instrument. He pulled his lip.

'Priapismic?'

Ray Doyle waited for just the right amount of time.

Then he buzzed Bodie and said, with deep pleasure: 'Look it up . . . It suits you.'

Then Doyle switched off again.

He was greatly amused.

Bodie's bafflement would last until he reached a dictionary. Although – that devil Ray Doyle! – Bodie had a damned good idea of what the old goat had been on about.

Bodie looked up at the light in the window of the apartment being used by the Ojukas. Ray was up there, and Bodie was down here. He checked his watch. He checked it again five minutes later, and then, watching the street, decided to wait at least twenty minutes before checking again.

Sixteen minutes later he looked at his watch, and made a face.

But the half hour went. The street remained quiet.

He called Doyle, and then, with a grunt of tiredness, got out of the car and headed for the door to the mansions.

The porch threw gaunt shadows, and the light was oddly indifferent; Bodie took that to be a mere part of the discreet nature of this place. He pressed the intercom buzzer on the heavy door. Up above, Doyle, expecting the call, answered the tone.

Down in the porchway the door clicked as it unlocked to Doyle's signal.

Bodie lifted his hand.

Something extraordinarily thin and extraordinarily hard wrapped itself around his neck.

He was being choked. He could not cry out.

A band of white-hot fire encircled his neck.

It felt as though his head was coming off, as though a cheese-wire was cutting through flesh and sinew and backbone, to topple his head off and roll it down the porch steps.

Two dark figures burst past Bodie as he was forcefully dragged back by the third man, who had the garrotte around his neck, choking him, hauling him back. The two men smashed past Bodie and started up the steps past the opened door.

The world was a miasma of blackness and darting specks of light, red and white, and Bodie's lungs laboured for air, his neck – he wasn't sure if he had a neck any more. He managed to get himself together and then let himself go into the formless, timeless, almost painless frenzy of pure action.

His elbow slogged back into the man's guts.

The fellow grunted and the garrotte around Bodie's neck loosened a fraction.

Bodie smashed again.

Now the dark figure reeled away, the end of the garrotte swinging wide, the wire and the cheese-cutter wooden grip spinning.

That was all Bodie needed.

He was on the dark hooded figure, chopping mercilessly, feeling cartilage and bone giving under the reflexive savagery of his attack.

The man went down.

Bodie left him, whirled for the door.

The door clicked locked even as his groping fingers touched it.

He was locked out, and Doyle was inside, on guard, expecting to see Bodie amble up the stairs – and instead his partner would meet two hooded gunmen head on.

As these hideous thoughts tumbled pell-mell through

Bodie's head he reached and drew his gun.

He blasted shots at the door lock.

Bodie opened the door with his revolver.

He went through the smashed open door on the heels of the bullets, bursting in and screaming up the stairs.

'Freeze!'

The two gunmen had almost reached the head of the stairs. They looked dark and ominous, hooded, their guns in their fists. The lower of the two whirled at Bodie's yell.

He shot as he turned, he shot with a wild desperation, he shot badly.

The slug pranged past Bodie's head, and the CI5 man put two into him. The gunman flopped down the stairs all arms and legs.

The smash of Bodie's door-opening brought Doyle to the head of the stairs.

He did not appear rubbing his eyes, half asleep, expecting to see his partner.

Ray Doyle appeared like a phantom rising from a battlefield. His gun was cocked between his two fists in the regulation grip, he was half-crouched, and as the top gunman shot, Doyle put three into him.

He flip-flopped down the stairs after his companion.

Gunsmoke hung on the air, acrid and bitter to the taste. The shattering crash of gunfire still reverberated up and down the stairs.

Bodie felt the pain of the garrotte around his neck, now. It hit him. He still stood, his gun lifted, and he felt his head might not – if he didn't nod – fall off.

Doyle let his revolver sag. Then, like a striking cobra, his fist whipped the revolver up.

He appeared to aim directly at Bodie.

Doyle yelled.

'Bodie!'

Bodie went down sideways as Doyle fired.

The slugs hit the man whom Bodie had put down. He'd snuck up on Bodie and now, as Doyle's bullets cut into him, he screeched and fell . . . His automatic pistol went off on full auto as his dying finger constricted. He sprayed the ceiling with slugs. The noise was overwhelming, and the stink of burnt powder gusted in, raw and gritty on the tongue.

Bodie looked at the fallen man; and Bodie looked very solemnly at him, very solemnly, indeed.

Then he turned his eyes up to his partner.

Doyle still stood in the aim, the revolver rock steady. It had been a little bit of fancy shooting, that. Not bad, considered Ray Doyle, not too bad, considering the indifferent light and the fool head of his partner in the way. Lucky, Bodie was, considered Doyle, lucky not to have ducked into a CI5 bullet.

Yes, a neat piece of tricky shooting . . .

Bodie nodded up at Doyle.

That nod summed it all up, that and the little crinkle of Bodie's lips.

Very calmly, Bodie said: 'I think I owe you one . . .'

Doyle snapped out of his silly self-congratulatory mood. He smiled, suddenly, relaxed, and he lowered his revolver.

''Course you do,' said Ray Doyle. 'One down, eight to go.'

Annoyed with himself for his lapse into being fancifully self-approving over a mere matter of shooting, when Bodie could be lying down at the foot of the stairs, filled with bullets, pumping blood, and dying, Doyle heard the footfall behind him. He turned at once, poised, to see Colonel Ojuka appear.

The pyjamas Okuja wore were of a resplendent fashion; but they were as nothing to the gorgeousness of the dressing gown he was just closing over them. The gold bullion tassels – flounders to the life – must have cost a fortune alone.

Doyle nodded curtly.

'A little more swift justice, Colonel. Getting to be quite a popular pastime, around you . . .'

Ojuka locked gazes with Doyle, but said nothing.

Truth to tell, there was little to say that was not more eloquently said by the bullet-tattered corpses of the men on the stairs.

Next day, bright and early, the partners shepherded their charge to CI5 HQ.

As usual, CI5 was located in a shabby old building, with a dusty, fusty, down-at-heel look. Most of the furniture could have come straight from an auction – probably it came from the rejects of Whitehall's Finest – and the carpets were thread bare. The facilities were rudimentary – except for the forensic laboratory and the communications centre and computer room and the garage. These were so super-modern and efficient they hurt the eye with their brightness.

Colonel Ojuka looked about with interest as they went through the building towards the meeting with Cowley.

Ojuka decided to make a little joke.

These two men detailed to protect him appeared to relish a joke as they shot would-be murderers down with ferocious efficiency.

'So,' said Colonel Ojuka. 'the nerve centre of CI5. Perhaps you should blindfold me.'

Bodie was matter-of-factly casual as he opened the door to the conference room.

'Not necessary, Colonel. You've already seen the nerve centre.' Casual, was Bodie, but there was that little curl to his lips as he spoke. 'We call it George Cowley.'

Cowley looked over inquiringly as the party entered. He looked over the top of his heavy horn-rimmed spectacles, and then took them off and waggled them by an ear piece. He did not waste time, after the ritual good mornings had been negotiated.

'You're a man who seems to have some very determined adversaries, Colonel Ojuka. And yet you say you have no idea who they could be.' He nodded to bring Bodie and Doyle to attention. 'The Colonel saw the bodies?'

'Yes, sir,' said Bodie. 'We're running checks on the weapons, and the car. Nothing yet.'

'The men were unknown to me,' said Ojuka. 'But I saw also that your men displayed great skill in turning them from adversaries into bodies. You train them well, Mister Cowley.'

'I train them to do their job. No more no less.' Cowley remained unimpressed by the Colonel's remark. 'And it would help me to do mine if you could give me a lead on where these attacks might be coming from.'

Ojuka moved his shoulders. 'The junta that has temporarily replaced me in Betan has not the strength to reach for me so determinedly in this country. It cannot be them.'

'Unless, of course, they've made some powerful friends in your absence. Or, at least, allies for the time being . . .'

Ojuka gave Cowley a quizzical look at this, and Cowley went on firmly.

'I've been looking at Betan quite closely, Colonel. You border on at least one power which includes neither your country nor mine in its sympathies.'

'And what does that imply to you?'

'A weak man,' said Cowley, 'in need of something will turn to a strong one to get it for him, if he can. If not by friendship, then by way of trade. Just as you are doing here.'

Ojuka's smile acknowledged the truth of Cowley's judgement.

'Well said. You understand the mechanics of the game, Mister Cowley. Do you have knowledge of such an alliance? It would interest me to hear it – '

'No, I don't.'

Bodie and Doyle caught the canniness in the old man's tone, and guessed that Ojuka wouldn't miss it, either.

'Even if I had,' went on Cowley, 'I understand the mechanics of the game well enough not to put too many cards in your hand, before tomorrow's conference.'

Now Ojuka laughed, exhibiting his admiration of Cowley's display of realpolitik, which, in Cowley's opinion, was as clever as eating ice cream in summer.

'I like you, Mister Cowley. I like you.'

The black face, filled with laughter, lined out, became hard, intense.

'So tell me what you propose to do with me.'

Cowley fiddled his glasses around, his sandy hair glinting golden under the overheads. Then he looked up, and this time the ice cream eating idea was seen in its true perspective; this time Cowley meant what he said.

'Simply to carry out my orders, which are to see you safely delivered to your conference.' He paused, and went on: 'I was instructed this morning that it's to be held at Gateways, in Sussex. Apparently the Foreign Office feel that such a meeting would arouse too much speculation, held openly here in London.'

Ray Doyle couldn't stop himself from interjecting: 'Might arouse some shooting, too, if yesterday's anything to go by.'

Cowley did not look at Doyle.

'I agree, Doyle. And when I want your comments I shall ask for them.'

He and Doyle both knew the effect this would have, and Cowley spoke to Ojuka more briskly.

'After last night's attempt, the flat provided by the FO is obviously unsafe. The police can provide adequate protection for Madame Ojuka; but I'm afraid I can't allow you to return there.'

'Then,' demanded the Colonel, 'where are you sending me? To the Tower of London?'

Still feeling Bolshie, Doyle muttered softly to Bodie: 'Not a bad idea . . :'

George Cowley just picked that up; but he chose to ignore damned insubordinate subordinates, and get on with sorting out this prickly Colonel.

'No, Colonel. We keep that for Her Majesty's prisoners. Not her guests.'

He made his small gesture to the partners.

'These two men will accompany you to Gateways today, and remain with you there until the conference is over. I understand you'll be leaving us after that.'

'Yes, indeed. A weak man must seek strong friends where he can find them. I'm sure you will agree.'

Smoothly, Cowley said: 'You'll know more about that than me. I'm no politician.'

Before Ojuka could digest the double-edged nature of the remark, Cowley swung on Bodie and Doyle.

'You two will draw weapons and communications equipment, as you think fit. Leave the Colonel with me, and you can do it now.'

As the partners obediently turned to move off, already listing weaponry they might need, Cowley slapped at them: 'I want minimum risk and a very low profile on this one. Is that clear?'

'Yes, sir,' said Bodie.

'Yes, sir,' said Doyle.

They went out, getting on with the mental listing of armaments, and Cowley, turning to Ojuka, suggested the interesting possibility of liquid refreshment.

Doyle walked along the corridor, mulling things over.

'Minimum risk,' he said, in his cuttingly sarcastic way. 'What's that supposed to mean, in this outfit?'

Bodie's lips curled.

'Trust in God – but if Ojuka's in the back seat take an Armalite and two stun-grenades before you go.'

Doyle smiled easily.

'Good thinking . . . '

That settled they walked on along the corridor. Mary walked past, going the other way, one of the more pretty secretaries around the place, a lady of decided views. One of her decided views was not to wear a brassiere. Going bra-less, she had been known to observe, indicated to all and sundry that a girl was not just a girl but a person.

Bodie and Doyle smiled appreciatively at Mary.

'I don't know,' observed Bodie, 'about low profile, though . . .'

'Who,' said Doyle, fervently, 'needs it?'

Chapter Five

Not courtesy alone dictated that Cowley should go around personally to see Madame Ojuka. Security would be that much more secure if he visited the scene of last night's shootings himself.

Kutunda opened the door and Cowley smiled warmly at her. That was easy enough, in all truth.

'Madame Ojuka. I hope I'm not disturbing you.'

'No. But where is my husband, Major Cowley? He is not with you?'

'No. I'm afraid not. That's why I called on you.'

Kutunda quizzed Cowley silently, her head a little on one side, watching him alertly.

'I spoke with Colonel Ojuka this morning. After last night's attempt on him, I'm afraid I couldn't allow him to return here again.'

'Why is that so, Major? You had given him protection here.'

'Yes, I had. But his whereabouts were obviously already known to his attackers, and I can't risk the chance of them trying a second time.'

'I see.' She eyed him. 'Then what have you done with him?'

'My men are taking him to the conference rendezvous in Sussex this morning.' Cowley smiled his easy smile again. His voice became plummier. 'He'll be a little early, of course; but in my view that's better than not being there at all.'

'Yes, of course.' Kutunda's brows drew down. 'He will be safe there? You will understand that his safety is of more concern to me than his – ambitions for the conference, Major Cowley.'

Cowley reassured her.

'I don't think you need worry, Madame Ojuka. Your husband's safety is also my first concern. And the two men he has with him are very competent.' He watched the expression on her face; she appeared to be reassured. 'Well, if you'll excuse me, I have an appointment to keep.'

She nodded, smiling somewhat hesitantly, still worried but less so than before Cowley's arrival.

'Thank you for calling, Major Cowley. It was kind of you.'

'Not at all. And try not to worry too much in the meantime. He's in good hands.'

Major Danby's information led to Cowley's next appointment. The ministry buildings stood in luxurious contrast to the starkness of CI5 HQ; but that was all frippery to George Cowley. He was shown up to see John Avery who by his dress and manner, the hint of silver at his temples, the shrewdness of his eyes, as much as by the acreage of carpet he enjoyed, was a senior member of the bureaucracy.

They shook hands in a formally polite way.

'Good of you to see me, Mr Avery.'

'Not at all. Take a seat, Major Cowley.' Avery himself sat at his desk, an erect, slender, polite but barracuda-like figure. 'Now – what can I do for you?'

'I'm making a report on the Ojuka situation for the Foreign Office. You're aware of what that situation is, of course – '

'Oh, yes. Our roving African warrior looking for some support from us. Quite a character, so I'm told.'

'He's certainly that.'

Cowley could remember enough in the past hours to reinforce that statement a hundred percent.

'I understand that the request for security on the visit he made yesterday came from this office. Is that so?'

Avery studied Cowley for a moment. Then: 'Yes, it did.' His manner was perfectly polite, not quite off-hand, but formally casual. 'Ojuka was kicking up a good deal of fuss about it, so the Minister decided to let him go – with instructions for a bodyguard, naturally.'

'And your office contacted Major Danby.'

'That's right.' Avery's manner was perfectly bland.

'Why did you not contact me at CI5? You must be aware that such a case is more suited to my men, than that of a retired military policeman – who happened to get himself shot down.'

Avery's manner became a little stiff at this.

'I'm aware of what took place yesterday, Cowley. A brave man died, in the course of his duty, and the Colonel was unharmed.'

Then Avery warmed up, leaning forward, making a small dismissive gesture. He was selling a bill of goods.

'To be quite frank with you, the notion of calling in CI5 for a school visit seemed akin to asking the SAS to rescue a cat out of a tree. Horses for courses, if you like.'

This sounded eminently logical; yet Cowley, very coolly, said: 'An error of judgement, then – on your part.'

This did not please John Avery at all. He stood up and began to pace the carpet, making Cowley imagine he was stalking these cats in trees he was maundering on about.

'It's easy to be wise after the event, Cowley. What you should remember is that nobody had any idea that Ojuka merited the sort of security that your department represents. As far as this office was concerned, he was a very small game. And I'm not going to be held responsible for any shortcomings on Major Danby's part . . .'

'Yes,' said Cowley. 'I can see that.'

He rose from the chair, turning towards the door.

'Thank you for your time, Avery. I'm sure there's nothing in your decision that you should worry about.' Now Cowley smiled the smile of the tiger. 'Or, if there is, I'll let you know about it.'

Cowley had reached the door when Avery replied. He kept his face averted as he spoke, but the suppressed anger in him was clear and palpable.

'Cowley – '

The chief of CI5 turned, his hand reaching for the door handle.

'Cowley – I understand he's yours now anyway. Take good care of him, won't you? Or you may find *yourself* being taken down a peg or two . . . '

The vehemence of the man puzzled Cowley. He realised that Avery was far more rattled over this business than he should be. Odd. Cowley smiled again, easily.

'Oh, yes, indeed. I'll do that.'

As the CI5 chief left, Avery glared after him, and that look was neither happy nor pleasant . . .

In his car Cowley pondered for a moment. But he was a man who covered all ends, and then went back to the middle. He chromium-plated his copper-bottoming.

He reached for the R/T –

'Alpha to base.'

When HQ answered, Cowley spoke precisely. He was well aware that the operator at the other end would pick up that firmness in his voice, and would pass the word along; the chief was on the prod.

'I want a full dossier on John Avery. Background, career history, the lot. One copy only, and given to me first hand. Understood?'

'Yes, sir,' said the Base operator.

Cowley's last barked 'Understood' elicited a responsive crack to the 'sir!'

With that, Cowley replaced the handset, started up and drove off, deeply pondering the situation, and wondering what those two rapscallions, the Bisto Kids, were up to.

At first the drive out into the Sussex countryside went smoothly and routinely. The Capri went well, Bodie drove, with Doyle at his side.

Colonel Ojuka sat in the back reading the *Financial Times*. He was engrossed in the paper.

More to be pleasant than anything else, Doyle said: 'Business, Colonel?'

Ojuka glanced up, and then back to the paper.

'A source of information.'

He crumpled the paper down, and expounded on his theories.

'The economies of the West are its true armies. Where the Soviets will send tanks and missile-launchers, the West will send soft drinks and denim trousers.'

Doyle knew about that. It was a wry set-up.

'And the Russians who build the tanks', he said, 'queue up in the black market for a pair of jeans.'

'Precisely.' Ojuka rustled his paper. 'It is informative to see behind the trenches in such a war.'

At the wheel, Bodie cricked his neck back.

'Can you tell who's winning?'

Ojuka laughed at this, delighted at his own acumen as much at Bodie's directness.

'Nobody! Because the makers of *all* these things must pour their money into the desert, or the sea – or threaten to fire it into the sky at each other. *That* is business . . . '

Refreshed by this salutary instruction period in elementary politico-economics, Ojuka returned to his paper.

Bodie and Doyle exchanged glances.

'He', said Bodie, 'has a point there – somewhere.'

'Well,' said Doyle, comfortably. 'It means you get your jeans made in Scotland, and all the Chinese ride bicycles.'

Bodie joined in.

'Which means if you buy a Japanese radio, all the mackerel are finished on the Isle of Wight.'

Doyle nodded and said with great profundity.

'That's business.'

Both partners agreed that this character Ojuka was a great character, silvered auto and all, *Financial Times* and all. Keeping him alive would be a real pleasure.

Bodie tooled the Capri out of suburban London, letting her feel her way, taking pleasure in the greenness of the countryside as they left the last gaggles of houses. The road stretched ahead. Trees began to be more than pallid dust covered objects and took on the regality of the countryside.

Ojuka looked out, frowning, his face intent.

'So many trees,' he said. 'So much fertility, in one little country . . . '

It had to be Bodie to say: 'Well, it rains a lot, for a little country.'

'Oh, yes, your weather. You talk always of the weather, as if there were some special meaning for the British, in the clouds, the sun.'

Doyle said: 'You don't get weather? What do you get?'

Ojuka's smile was a trifle rueful.

'In my country, the weather kills you, or it does not. At noon, the desert rock will blister you; at night, they crack like rifles as they freeze. What is there to say of such weather?'

'You don't make it sound like a tourist trap.'

'Allah be praised, it is not. It is a country for Africans, and I will not leave it to the grey mercies of some puppet regime. I shed blood to rule it, and I shall do so again.'

Bodie glanced into the rear view mirror not with the automatic reflex of the driver to check his situation on the road; but to look at Ojuka. He caught something on the back trail that took his attention. He nodded across to Doyle to check the second mirror, for Bodie wasn't going to shift the driver's mirror for the benefit of the passenger.

'Keep your lovely eyes on that Merc,' he said to Doyle in a quiet voice.

He hauled the Capri out of the intermittent traffic onto the fast lane. The country fled past, trees and hedges, telephone poles and fences blurring. The wind whistled.

Doyle checked his mirror.

The big Mercedes hauled out into the fast lane as they had done, tagged on. Doyle nodded.

'We've still got him.'

'I', stated Bodie with emphasis, 'thought my neck was itching.'

'Can't tell from here,' said Doyle, trying to check the occupants of the following car. 'Two at least.'

Colonel Ojuka sensed the change of mood.

He rustled the *Financial Times* away and leaned forward.

'We are being followed?'

'Looks like it, Colonel.' Doyle shifted in his seat, trying to spot the following car more clearly. 'Whoever these people are, you're definitely not their flavour of the month.'

Ojuka laughed at this in his easy, feline way, and then rapped out: 'You will give me my gun?'

'I might', Doyle told him, 'as well give you my head on a plate.' He spoke formally. 'No, sir. I cannot return your weapon.'

'A pity.' Ojuka relaxed into the back seat. 'Then the matter is in your hands.'

'All right.' Bodie took another perspective of the Mercedes in the rear view mirror. 'We'll see how serious they get. Keep your head down, Colonel.'

In the next instance the car lunged forward as Bodie pressed the accelerator. He took the Capri forward in a smooth rush, building speed fast and powerfully, hurled her off the main arterial road with its traffic and into the network of minor roads criss-crossing the countryside.

No time to stop and admire the scenery now, no time to sniff the fragrance of blooms, taste the sweetness on the country air. Time now only to hang on, to sway with the motion of the car as Bodie hurled her around the bends, taking a Grand Prix line, haring on, belting hell-for-leather flat out.

And the Mercedes screamed after them

The big car lurched dangerously on the sharp corners, gained and lost distance, swinging heavily along after them.

Doyle braced himself in the seat, looked back.

He broke the news to his partner.

'I got news for you . . . They're serious.'

They fleeted under an overhanging canopy of beech, whirled on into the light beyond. The road unwound like a ribbon. The Mercedes kept coming. Bodie recognised that whoever was driving the big car was a master. But, then, so was Master Bodie . . .

The occupants of the front seats of the Mercedes were both big men, well-tanned, with hard faces. The fierce chase went on, and the gap opened and narrowed.

Then Bodie hit a straight stretch, and the pursuing car clung like a leech.

The Mercedes's passenger leaned from his open side window.

The gun was big, bulking in his fist, even though it was a sidearm. He took steady aim.

Doyle, looking back, saw that ominous humped shape at the window, saw the menace. He dived for his own gun, and bellowed at Ojuka.

'Get down!'

The man chasing them fired three shots.

Obediently, the Colonel dropped flat.

But Doyle couldn't get his gun into action before at least one of the shots ripped into the rear tyre.

The tyre blew.

The Capri slewed, dancing crazily across the road as Bodie fought the controls.

The noise of crashing and banging, the scream of tortured tyres, the feel of uncontrolled motion, drove wedges of scarlet into Bodie's head; but he had to fight this wheel, get the speeding car back again under control and –

The Capri slewed end-to-end, spun again, went off the road and, hopping the ditch with the front end, finished half on her side and half in a praying-Mantis position.

The sounds of banging and crashing were joined by the sounds of breaking glass.

The two men in the following Mercedes felt, no doubt, confident.

The driver brought the big car to a halt on the road by the crashed Capri.

The two men were, indeed, big and tough and hard. They jumped out. Both carried guns. They advanced on the wreck of the Capri. They could see the driver, wedged in his seat.

The men levelled their guns at the sprung open door. Shakily, Colonel Ojuka emerged. He looked dizzy.

The guns menaced him, and their owners were quite confident. There was no arguing with those levelled weapons. The tanned faces carried looks of grim determination. Smiling just a trifle, Colonel Ojuka passively raised his hands . . .

The hot stink of burned rubber where the Capri had skidded in her wild slewing rush at the end hung on the air. The smell of oil and petrol indicated this was no place to hang about, or strike a light, or shoot a gun.

Trapped at the wheel, Bodie squirmed and fought to get free.

And Colonel Ojuka, still smiling, raised his hands high . . .

The two tanned men closed in . . .

Moving with lethal speed, crouched, tensed, his revolver snouting, Ray Doyle erupted from the far side of the car. He'd scrambled out into concealment, and now he burst into the action like a Spitfire screaming down onto the tails of a pair of bumbling Stukas.

He shot in a fast and accurate flow, controlled shooting, and yet he was moving all the time and presenting a fleeting target. The shots from the weapons of the tanned men flew wide.

Ray Doyle's slugs hit their marks with unerring accuracy.

The men screeched and flopped. Both were dead, with scant heartbeats after they were hit. Doyle's shooting was efficient and ruthless.

Colonel Ojuka lowered his raised hands.

He beamed. He beamed at Ray Doyle.

Then he looked down on the two dead men.

'Excellent, my friend, excellent. Should you ever wish it, there is a place for you beside me, in Betan.'

Doyle spoke drily.

'No thanks, Colonel. I'm too fond of our peaceful English countryside.'

He looked around at the road, the fence, the ditch, the panorama of trees, and then at the grotesquely twisted bodies of the gunmen.

'Fresh air, green trees, the birds singing over the crash of gunfire.'

A noise reminiscent of an ancient gas-boiler water-heater approaching eruption point bubbled from the car.

Doyle swung about, holstering his revolver.

Bodie bellowed: 'Hey! Are you going to help me out of here, or do I have to wait for the RAC?'

Doyle gave his partner the benefit of a long, thoughtful silence. He walked across and looked down into the driving seat. Bodie was stuck, stuck good.

Doyle shook his head, and pursed up his lips.

'Come on! Come on!'

Finally, Doyle condescended to start to assist, and struggled to free his partner.

'I think,' he said, straining away, 'you might have lost your insurance credibility here.'

'No,' said Bodie. 'No. I'm covered. Third party, fire, and shoot-outs.'

That summed up Bodie, true to the life.

Doyle got him free and he scrambled out of the wreck, started dusting himself off in his fastidious way.

Doyle said: 'What now?'

Bodie winced and began massaging a bruise.

'You heard what the man said. Minimum risk, low profile . . . Which means not waiting around here to make an accident report.'

Doyle agreed; but he was staring calculatingly at Ojuka. 'Colonel – whoever wants you is on the inside. And very close. That pair didn't just pick us up out of the rush hour.'

'That is true.' Ojuka's frown indicated he was puzzled and annoyed. 'And whoever it is, also works on *your* side. Your government made these arrangements, not I. It would seem, gentlemen – ' And here Colonel Ojuka smiled his dazzling white smile. ' – I have enemies everywhere.'

'He's right,' said Doyle as he and Bodie put their heads together by the stern of the smashed Capri. Ojuka was again staring at the dead men. 'Every security set-up's leaked like an old tin bath so far. We can't even trust standing orders.'

'All right,' agreed Bodie. 'Let's override 'em. Special Case Situation. We don't even know if Gateways is safe for him, so we can forget about standing orders, can't we?'

'And?' said Doyle, helpfully prodding.

'Go to cover, and stay there until we know different. Hotel, inn, or something. Random choice. That way, no leaks.'

The decision that Bodie was right did not take Doyle long. 'We've got the scrambler phone. We'll call Cowley when we're holed up, but not before. Let's move.'

Bodie jerked a comprehensive thumb at what was left of his car.

'We aren't going to get very far in that thing.'

Ray Doyle's pragmatic answer was to ' pick up their equipment from the wreck and then, followed by Bodie, walk to the Mercedes.

'I know – you don't mind driving a foreign car for a change, do you? They're not in a rush for it.'

The dossier the CI5 Intelligence section prepared on John Avery was thorough, detailed, interesting. Cowley took the file from Murphy in the CI5 Computer Room. Murphy, the mountaineer on the team, spoke briskly.

'The dossier on Avery you asked for, sir. It's fairly comprehensive.'

'Good work, Murphy.' Cowley flicked the file open and perching on the edge of a desk started to browse through.

Murphy could read nothing in the old man's expression.

'What's it all about, sir? You don't ask for a coded file on one of our own, every day of the week.'

Cowley, reading and absorbed, answered in a way he

probably would not have done had he not had his attention directed elsewhere.

'No, I don't. But when I called on John Avery he was rattled about something – more than he should have been over a routine visit from CI5.'

'You think he's doubling on us?'

'I wish I knew. But I do know this much. Somebody is very close to us on Ojuka. And with CI5 responsible for him, I intend to find out who – because it's our neck on the block if we lose him.'

The way Cowley spoke gave Murphy the shivers.

The chief was still checking through the file as the evening wore on, trying to dig out facts that were not there, or hidden, concealed truths behind the bald history. The phone rang.

Mary handed the phone across, and Cowley took it, a preoccupied smile enough thanks.

'Cowley . . . ' The distant voice began to tell him startling things.

'What?'

After a moment, when the salient facts had been taken in, he snapped: 'How long ago was this? I see . . . You still have the man who found the car, the bodies? All right. Hold him. Yes, hold him. He's to talk to nobody. And give me total silence on this until I say otherwise. Yes, Inspector, *my* responsibility.'

The phone slammed back on its cradle.

For an instant Cowley's face looked that of the Lord God of Thunders, preparing to destroy cities.

Then he rasped at Mary: 'Get Murphy back here on the double.'

Mary's bra-less body jumped and her rhythm changed. Cowley saw none of that; he could see a country road and a smashed car and dead bodies, and spilling trails of blood – and he could not see his two prize agents or their charge.

'Tell Murphy he's on call. Priority One . . . '

'Yes, sir,' said Mary, and swung into action.

*   *   *

92

The Mercedes boomed along the country roads, and whilst Bodie still drove in Sussex, he no longer headed for Gateways. Doyle, alongside, rummaged in the glove compartment. Ojuka, as usual, sat in the back.

Bodie said: 'You recognise either of those two, Colonel?'

'Only as dead men, Mister Bodie. They were not known to me.'

'Nothing in here to give them away, either,' said Doyle, his hands in the glove compartment. 'Probably a hire car.'

'It's a stolen car right now,' pointed out Bodie.

'Let's just say requisitioned,' Doyle half-turned, forgetting the glove compartment. He spoke to Ojuka, and his tone indicated the questions he wanted answered.

'I'll tell you one thing about them. They wanted you alive. If they were going to kill you, you'd have been dead when you got out of the car back there, hands up or no hands up . . . '

The calmness of Colonel Hakim Ojuka was admirable; but Doyle could see the trouble in the man.

'All of us walk on the precipice of our fate, Mister Doyle. If I am alive, it is because Allah wills it.'

Doyle absorbed this and turned back to face forward, saying in an aside to Bodie at the wheel: 'I wonder if Cowley's realised that yet?'

'Don't know.' Bodie turned the wheel gently as they rounded a curve in the road. The shadows were dropping down and the hedgerows and trees were more black than green. Lights showed ahead, and the loom of a house. 'There – what do you think?'

They passed a badly-illuminated signboard.

They had time to make out the name.

ASHCROFT HOTEL.

Then Bodie slowed the Mercedes and they could see the hotel, lighted windows, the RAC and AA signs, parked cars in front, a quiet, normal evening English scene.

'Yes,' said Doyle. 'Good as any. If Cowley's got word of the car the sooner we call him the better.'

Bodie nodded agreement and swung the big car towards the hotel, crunched up the drive between white painted gates. The place was low and rambling, with ivy across the walls, and wooden settles outside. It was half-and-half an ancient hostelry and a modern hotel unit. Bodie parked and Doyle collected the suitcase and shoulder bag he had taken into his care. Ojuka joined them and they headed for the hotel entrance, where coloured light spilled from tinted window glass, and the distant sound of voices and – even – the clink of glasses gave a welcome.

The clink of glasses was probably entirely imaginary. But it fitted the welcoming mood of this quiet place.

Inside the lobby was a good quality carpet, and polished wooden furniture and a grandfather clock, the receptionist at the shining counter was speaking on the phone. As Bodie walked up she hung up and turned with a smile. She was, Bodie did not fail to notice, rather pretty.

'Good evening – can I help you?'

Bodie's charm radiated warmly.

'I hope so. We'd like a double and a single room adjoining, if that's possible.' The smell of cooking invaded Bodie's nostrils most pleasantly. It was a good, crisp, fresh scent, redolent of appetizing dinners. Bodie felt the hollowness of his insides. His smile broadened. 'I'm afraid we didn't have the opportunity to make a reservation – couple of things came up – and we had to make a detour . . . Found ourselves here.'

'Yes, I see.' The receptionist opened the register, its leather cover well-polished and showing signs of long wear. 'I'll just check for you. Will you be staying long?'

'No, I shouldn't think so. Just overnight, probably.'

During this Doyle and Ojuka had remained in the background, looking about. Now Doyle, smiling easily, stepped up.

'Depends on what the boss says. We're – er – travellers in – tropical fish.' He half-turned to take in Ojuka, whose black face looked calm and impassive. 'Mr Guppy here is our overseas buyer. *Very* important man to us.'

94

Not only the receptionist took this in with some interested amusement; Bodie suspected his partner was feeling light in the head. But, still and all, it made a more colourful cover than an ordinary routine tale ever would . . .

'Well,' said the receptionist when she'd run her finger down the book's tally. 'I think we can accommodate you. Yes – yes, nine and ten are adjoining. It's usually taken as a children's room; but the bed is full size. There's no bathroom, I'm afraid; but there's a shower. Would that suit you?'

'Very nicely.' Bodie sniffed that delectable aroma of dinner. He spoke drily, half to Doyle. 'I'm sure Mr Guppy won't mind if the wallpaper's got ducks on it. Would you, Mr Guppy?'

The face that Ojuka turned to them bore puzzlement. The partners could not afford to crease up now; but they felt like it. Minding Ojuka, looking out for the new Mr Guppy, had its rewarding moments, as well as its bloody ones . . .

Murphy checked out the forensics with the doctor and learned that the bullets prised out of the dead bodies had come from CI5 issue. Logically, then, there had been a shoot out. As Murphy said, drily: 'If the dead men hit anything it didn't fall over.'

One of the corpses had yielded a bracelet made of elephant hair. Murphy studied this intently. The doctor also advised him that the tans the men were wearing had most certainly not been acquired in England and Africa came up as a possibility, coupled with the elephant hair bracelet.

Then Murphy checked out the man who had discovered the car and the bodies and who was now unwillingly held in the local nick. He turned out to be a traveller in fruit machines, and the very shakiness of his own position ensured he could be guaranteed not to make a fuss.

Then Murphy reported in to Cowley.

He rang from the station, and Cowley took the call in CI5 HQ's Computer Room.

'Three seven's car, all right, sir,' said Murphy, 'offside rear wing and tyre show bullet damage, compatible with a gun found on one of the bodies.'

'And Bodie? Doyle? Colonel Ojuka?'

'No sir, no trace of them – apart from four five's ammunition in the corpses.'

'So,' said Cowley. 'So they've either been taken or they've gone to ground with him. What about the two dead? Any identification?'

'Nothing tangible, sir. One of them was wearing an African bracelet. And they either had sun-lamps, or they hadn't been long in this country.'

'Is that so?' Cowley stared at the dossier on John Avery, open before him. 'All right. Get prints and photographs and get them to Records. And make damn sure that Inspector keeps his security tight down there. We're running blind, until we know where Ojuka is. Stay on call.'

When Cowley replaced the phone he picked up the dossier. He sat, looking at it, turning the bits and pieces around in that shrewd head of his . . .

Colonel Ojuka, relaxed in the easy chair, found much to interest, amaze and baffle him in the copy of *Country Life* he was reading. He was polite about his amusement at the antics, though. In their room Doyle was making sure his weapon was free of dust, grit and dirt, was bright clean and slightly oiled, and was fully reloaded with ammo. The gun gleamed blued-steel hard in the subdued lighting.

Bodie had the little suitcase open on the bed and was connecting up the scrambler and phone device. He had no feelings of super-spy doing this, for he was well aware that these kits were freely available in the US market. He was chatting away to his partner as he worked, and he spoke with a fine free scorn.

'Tropical fish . . . Where'd you get *that* one from?'

'First thing that came to mind,' said Doyle. 'I had a tank

full of them one time, when I was a kid. Angel fish, guppys, all sorts. Pretty little things.' The cartridge in his finger glittered as he snapped it in. 'Until the cat got in and went fishing . . .'

'Yeah? You should have kept a couple of piranhas in there to look after them.'

'Yeh.' Doyle looked up. 'Like us.'

Bodie jerked his head in Ojuka's direction.

'That's no angel fish, that's a full grown barracuda.' He finalised the last connection and gave the set a little pat. 'All right. We're set.' He punched buttons, methodically, carefully. He spoke clearly into the phone. 'Three seven to Alpha One. Repeat, three seven to Alpha One.'

The call, scrambled into incomprehensible bits and pieces, fled over the airwaves and CI5 HQ picked up on the call. Bodie smiled.

'Bingo,' he said to Doyle.

At CI5 HQ Mary, back on duty, popped out of the door and spotted Cowley prowling about along the corridor.

'Sir – there's an R/T call coming in on seven-seven.' She drew a breath and a passing clerk almost dropped his file. 'That's Bodie and Doyle's channel, sir.'

Galvanised, Cowley leaped for the phone.

'Put me through, Mary.' He snatched up the receiver and went on at a rate of knots. 'Alpha. Where in *hell* are you? Is Ojuka safe?'

Bodie's voice rode the airwaves, and scrambled and unscrambled though it might be, Cowley could clearly detect that typical Bodie smugness at a job well done.

'Yes, sir, he's safe. We've got him at the Ashcroft Hotel, near Reigate. We pulled some attention on the road which must have been from the inside. So we went for cover. There's a leak on this one, sir. A leak as big as your fist.'

'Aye, I know it.' Cowley fought the tiredness back. 'And I think I know where from, and why, so let's keep Ojuka there until we have the key to this.'

'As long as we're untraced, Ojuka's safe enough here.'

'Right,' said Cowley. 'Now listen to me.' He took a breath, and it all added together, quite neatly, and quite groundlessly if they'd got it wrong.

'John Avery at the Home Office has got more interests in African finance than you've got in air hostesses. And he's acting *very* jumpy. He's also got a house in Sussex, which practically overlooks Gateways. A place called Beechcroft, about ten miles off the Reigate Road. I want you to get down there and stake it out, Bodie. And stick to it like glue until this conference is under way. Understood?'

'Yes, sir. I don't see the connection, though – '

'You don't have to. Just bear in mind that the two men you killed this afternoon were white Africans – brought in to take Ojuka. If this is coming from the inside, Avery's got the motive *and* the place to do it from. Meanwhile, Doyle will take care of the Colonel.'

Cowley cut the connection on that, not wishing to have to stand for any more of Bodie's wilful Bolshie behaviour; of course the connections were tenuous, and of course he could be all wrong and of course Avery could be lily-white. But, but George Cowley, too, had a nose for villains . . .

Bodie put the phone down and looked philosophically at Doyle.

'Looks like you're guarding the tank on your own, angel-fish. I'm on surveillance for the night.'

Doyle frowned.

'Who?'

'John Avery. Our very own undersecretary.'

Doyle was incredulous. 'Avery? Where does he fit in?'

Bodie stood up, already starting to act on the chief's instructions.

'Right in the middle, according to Cowley. Says he's got a lot of naughty money in Africa, and sweat on his upper lip about it. And a country house half-way between here and Gateways.'

He dumped the shoulder bag's contents and began to sort the gear, tossing ammo clips at Doyle.

'Here – don't eat 'em all at once.'

The bullets glistened silver and the cartridge cases glistened gold.

'No,' said Doyle. 'I'll chew 'em slowly. So – where's the connection?'

'Those two cowboys you took out this afternoon were white Africans – imported – if that's who's going for Ojuka, they could be using Avery's place as a springboard.'

Doyle thought about this development.

'Yeh, they could. But that still doesn't put Avery as close to Ojuka as they've come. That pair were inside Cowley's *own* security today.' Doyle picked up one of the ammoclips for the rifle, and tossed it in his hand. 'He's gambling.'

Bodie was on his way.

'So I'm on surveillance.' He nodded towards Ojuka's room. 'Don't let the cat get at him, will you?'

'No chance,' said Doyle. 'I was upset enough last time . . .'

But Bodie was gone.

Chapter Six

After Colonel Hakim Ojuka had relieved Ray Doyle of just about all his spare cash, Doyle dumped his last hand, mightily miffed.

'Aces and kings, Mister Doyle,' said Ojuka, raking in his winnings under the lamplight. 'Black ones.'

'That's four in a row.'

'Again?' Ojuka riffled the pasteboards.

Doyle stared morosely at the shrunken pile of silver before him on the table. He sniffed.

'Yeh, okay. I haven't much left to lose.'

Ojuka dealt. He said: 'Then we are well matched.'

Doyle caught the implication clearly enough.

'What do you think makes them want you so badly, then?'

'Because I am a symbol to my people.' Ojuka spoke evenly and with a calm force that drove meaning into his every word. This was a man, Doyle saw, possessed by the demon of mission. 'Because whilst I live, the junta can have no true power in Betan. They know I shall return, to prise their fingers from my country.'

And Ray Doyle met that evenness with a calmness of his own that told Colonel Ojuka that a backbone of steel stiffened the man opposite – if he hadn't already realised that by what Doyle had done so far.

'From what I can make out,' said Doyle. 'You weren't exactly spotless when *you* took it. Firing squads, mass round-ups ... You must have made yourself some enemies.'

Ojuka rode the implications coming at him in his usual calm and impressive manner. His brows drew down a fraction, true; but he met Doyle's attack head on.

'That is true. But which of us is spotless on the road to power? The people fear me, but they know me as one of them, and thus they love me. When I travel through my country, they chant for *me*. O-JU-KA! O-JU-KA!' As he chanted this out Doyle caught a flashing glimpse of the rows and ranks and immense fields of chanting people, all black and shining with fervour, all chanting away for this man opposite. It was a sobering thought, something to make King Solomon's Mines leap out in perspective.

'But,' Ojuka continued, hard and bitter now. 'These men behind their masks, they do not chant for them. That is why Ojuka is dangerous to them.'

The real power of this man came over then. They finished up the hand and disposed of the last of Doyle's silver, and then he decided to take a shower. Ojuka settled down with a magazine, stretched on the bed, and then threw the magazine aside. He was not settled at all. He stared at the bedside phone.

The sound of running water from the connecting shower reassured him. He reached for the phone and swiftly dialled out a familiar number.

Kutunda answered the phone herself.

When she realised who was ringing her at this hour she woke up to a quivering alertness.

'Hakim! Where are you? What has happened?' She listened as Ojuka sketched in the details. 'But you are safe now? You will stay there?'

'Yes, until tomorrow. Then I shall be taken to the conference. I am weary of delays, and hiding. Kutunda, when it is settled, you will join me. Already I miss you.'

Kutunda's face showed an expression at variance with her words as she replied. 'And I miss you, Hakim. I am glad you thought to speak to me. Yes – goodbye, Hakim.'

She put the phone down, Her face set into hard, hating lines, ridged. She looked across the room of the flat she had shared with her husband, to Faroud.

Faroud nodded, impassively. He was a large, dark man, heavily-set, wearing European clothing, and yet redolent of the mysteries of Africa. He carried the aura of a caged black cheetah, chained but deadly, waiting . . .

'Interesting. He has succeeded admirably in avoiding us so far. I think it is time to pay a call upon our ally in this matter . . . '

George Cowley would have been immensely interested to see just what office was visited by Faroud. At night there was a certain difference in feel to the ministerial furnishings; John Avery filled his office with his presence. Faroud was not impressed. Things were supposed to have been done, and these things had not been accomplished.

'So it would seem he has escaped you once again, Mr Avery. And soon it will be too late. Once an agreement is reached with your government, he will have influence and power and we shall never stop him.'

'I trust you're not blaming me, Mr Faroud.' Avery sounded tough; but there was bluster in the man. 'I can't answer for the failings of our mutual friends. I act simply as a go-between for your interests and theirs, nothing more.'

'That is true; but I understand their influence over your own interests is considerable, is it not? Any failure here will certainly reflect badly upon yourself, even disastrously, Mister Avery.'

Avery had no answer to this uncomfortable home truth. He took up the main thread again.

'And you say Madame Ojuka knows where he is now?'

'Yes. He has spoken with her this evening.'

'I sometimes think,' said Avery, very aware of the coiled menace of Kutunda, 'that Madame would happily accomplish your task herself, if she were asked to.'

'That would solve her personal grievance, no doubt. But we who rule Betan are most anxious that justice is *seen* to be done to Colonel Ojuka.'

'Then,' said Avery, nodding agreement, 'we shall have to try harder, won't we. And, with her assistance, once again, I think . . . '

So saying, Avery reached for the phone and dialled the

discreet if not dingy hotel where Parker was putting up.

Parker answered at once. He was a heavy man, heavy of face and heavy of shoulder, blue-chinned, tough, and he spoke with the trace of a voortrekker accent.

'Yes? I see,' he said as Avery broke the bad news. 'What the hell went wrong? All right, all right. This time – I go myself. Where is he?'

Avery passed on the location, supplied by Faroud from Kutunda, given by Ojuka himself to his wife.

'Okay, we'll be there. You just make sure the pick-up stands for tomorrow.'

Parker slammed the phone down and glared around balefully at Moon, standing lumpishly waiting for orders. Moon, as a henchman, supplied more muscle in the operation.

'They lost him,' Parker told him. 'And they paid for it. Get Davis, and bring the car. We've got one more chance.'

In CI5 HQ Computer Room George Cowley sifted through the details of his night's paperwork when Murphy came in with the file requested from Records.

'Anything there?'

'Not much, I'm afraid, sir,' said Murphy. 'One of them fits a description we have on some mercenary activity over there; but no positive ID.'

'Well, he was in the right trade, if nothing else. No link-up with any of Avery's concerns?'

'Not from this end . . . '

'And yet he's in it up to his neck, I'll swear to it.' Cowley knew he was right; but he had to prove it not least to himself, first. He tapped the file. 'Look at this. Three directorships in the past ten years, of companies with mining interests in Africa. Investments in heavy engineering, mineral surveys, transport franchise . . . All in areas under the jurisdiction of Betan.'

'Well, he wouldn't be the first to make a fortune out of someone else's back garden, would he?'

'Not by a long way. But he's bringing it out through the

next-door neighbour's – and if *they* turn against him, Avery loses everything.'

Murphy pursed up his lips.

'You think he's trading Ojuka with them, for some goodwill?'

'Aye, I do. But I can't pull a man of Avery's weight in for what I *think* he's doing. We've got to find a connection on him, before we can touch him.' He mulled this knotty problem over. 'What bothers me is how he's been getting inside us as he has.'

Murphy nodded agreement to this. 'Every time ... Ojuka might as well be telling them what he's up to himself.'

That old look of smoky battle in Cowley's eyes made Murphy guess the chief had hooked into something. Cowley nodded with slow meaning.

'Yes, he might as well be. And we've been so damned sure of him, we haven't been looking close enough to home.' At Murphy's expression, Cowley said: '*His* home. I think it's time we looked into Madame Ojuka's eyes on this one . . .'

That lady herself sat behind the wheel of her car in a country layby as the heavy form of Parker climbed in and flopped down in the passenger seat. The day had dawned, and the birds had sung, and no doubt the grass had risen a millimetre or two. But Parker and Kutunda had their minds on matters of ugly weight . . .

'You're a very prompt lady,' said Parker, at the rendezvous point on the dot. 'I like that.'

'What,' said Kutunda with a coldly metallic snap in her voice, 'you like or dislike is of no concern to me. I came to see you do not fail again.'

Parker eased his breath. 'Just get through the door, lady. That's all you've got do.'

The car pulled out, followed by a second with the henchmen. Parker intended to make it quick and cool and deadly this time. This time it would stick because he was there in person. Kutunda shared exactly the same sentiments.

Cowley's call on Madame Ojuka's flat was by some time too late. He spoke to the plain-clothes detective planted on duty outside. This worthy was nonplussed by Cowley's vehemence.

'Out?' said Cowley. 'Are you telling me you just let her walk out of here, Sergeant?'

'Well – yes, sir. My orders were simply to guard the building, sir, not to detain her. She's not under arrest . . . '

Cowley fumed; he fumed silently, but the detective sergeant was under no illusions; he could all but see the steam rising. Then –

'And she gave you no indication of where she was going?'

'No, sir. I assumed it was something to do with Mr Avery's call last night – '

'Avery was *here*? Are you sure?'

'Quite sure, sir. I checked his security pass when he arrived.'

'What', said Cowley, 'did he want with Madame Ojuka?'

The detective-sergeant was too old a hand to be caught on that one. 'Not my business to guess, sir. And I don't go in for button-holing government figures for the fun of it . . . '

Cowley looked away, looked at the street, looked back.

'No, Sergeant. I suppose you don't.'

He and Murphy took their departure, heading back for the car.

'If Avery's been here, we're on to something.'

They reached the car and climbed in. 'Let's hope,' Cowley said with fervour, 'they're not.'

He yanked up the R/T and called out.

'Alpha to base . . . Has four five called in yet? No . . . When he does, tell him we're on our way down, and not to make one move until we get there, whatever Ojuka might say.' He stopped, thought, and added harshly: 'Or his wife.'

The Rover three and a half wheel-spun and then screeched away, heading fast for the open road and Sussex.

Whilst Bodie's uncomfortable vigil outside Avery's Sussex house continued, Doyle and Ojuka readied themselves for the coming day. Bodie had spotted a large and heavily-set black man enter Avery's house, and docketed the information away. If things were to break, then this would be the time and place for them, he fancied.

At the Ashcroft Hotel Doyle was about to call in on the portable scrambler phone.

A light knock rapped against the outer door.

Doyle looked up, as Ojuka emerged from the adjoining room.

'Hallo?' said Doyle.

He unholstered his revolver and moved to the door.

Kutunda's voice came from outside.

'Mr Doyle? May I speak with my husband, please?'

At the sound of that smooth pleasant voice Colonel Ojuka beamed with enormous pleasure.

'Kutunda!'

Doyle saw Ojuka open the door. The woman walked in, gracefully, with a lithe swing, and Ojuka embraced her.

'You – ?' said Doyle. Then, to Ojuka: 'Wait a minute – you *told* her . . . '

He had no chance to go on.

The door smashed fully open. Parker and his hefty henchmen burst in. But they did not bust their way in alone.

Doyle's instinctive reaction with his weapon froze.

These swine had the pretty receptionist, tied up and gagged, bustled along in front of them. She was used as a shield against Doyle's bullets. Also, Parker had his gun thrust cruelly into the girl's neck, and by the expression on the ugly man's face, Doyle knew the fellow would have no compunction in using his gun on the receptionist.

'Leave it!' shouted Parker, as Doyle thought again and brought his gun up, perhaps to try a side shot. Parker

106

twisted the girl's head up, so that his gun barrel dinted in the pink skin to a concave whiteness.

'I said leave it!'

Ojuka stood to one side, covered by the gun of Moon, and Davis had a two-handed aim on Doyle.

Parker gloated.

'On the floor!'

Doyle's face was a cold mask of hatred as he dropped his revolver.

But Colonel Ojuka stared and stared at his wife.

'Yes, Hakim,' she said, and her voice lashed him with triumphant contempt. 'Me!'

The restraining bonds of reason snapped for Ojuka then and, like an enraged bull, he launched himself at Kutunda.

Moon lifted his gun and brought the heavy barrel down in a crashing blow to Ojuka's head.

Ojuka went on and down, smashing into the floor, out cold.

Terrified, her eyes rolling, the receptionist chose this moment to lash out. Her legs flailed as she kicked at Parker. The gunman staggered with her weight on him.

Doyle ducked, knocked aside the gun covering him, went on in a strong smooth flow of action to smash into Parker. He was there; he had the fellow to rights –

The gun barrrel that sledged down on Doyle's head stretched him out on the carpet alongside Ojuka.

The receptionist, momentarily freed, made a panic-stricken rush for the door and Parker shot her as she ran.

'No!' screamed Kutunda.

Shaking with anger, the gun trembling in his fist, Parker rounded on her. His face looked mad with passion.

'Shut your mouth, lady. You got what you came for.'

Moon stepped up, aimed his gun at Doyle, his finger white on the trigger.

'No,' said Parker, harsh and dominating. He felt his jaw where one of Doyle's blows had half-landed. 'I owe him. I want him wide awake when he gets his . . . '

Ojuka and Doyle were dragged up by the scruffs of their

necks and some kind of sense shaken back into them. Their hands were bound and then Parker and his gang shepherded them out of the room. Kutunda followed.

A hotel guest, startled by the crash of gunfire, popped an enquiring head out onto the corridor. Parker did not hesitate. His gun cracked out, splintering the architrave of the door, and the guest, shaken out of his wits, ducked back. The woodwork splintered under the impact of the big bullet, gashed raw against the sombre paintwork.

Through the lobby the procession was led by Kutunda, heading determinedly towards the doors and outside and the car park. Parker's gun menaced any enquiring guests.

'Stay back!' he warned them. 'Back!'

Outside they stormed towards the parked cars, and Ojuka was heaved into the back of the car containing Kutunda and Moon. Barely conscious, Doyle was bundled into the back of the other car with Davis, as Parker dived behind the steering wheel.

With a screech of spinning tyres and sprays of flung gravel, the cars roared away.

The pain in Colonel Ojuka's head did not lessen; but he had a tough skull and was used to taking life's knocks. He stirred, painfully, and Kutunda turned to look down at him. Ojuka returned her steady gaze . . .

'Why, Kutunda? What have these dogs paid you?'

'Nothing, Hakim, except the promise that when you are returned to Betan, they will cut off your head, for all to see.'

The fanatical grimness of Kutunda's words, instead of driving Ojuka back, brought a macabre smile to his face. Her sincerity amused him as a man might be amused by the antics of a monkey on the brink of the grave.

'That would seal their power for them, certainly. But for *you* . . . ?'

Now Kutunda's face and voice became cold with a deadly chill. 'It will pay for the lives and the land you took when you took me. I have lived for it since then; as have others. And they will see you pay, with your blood.'

The sheer irrelevance of this revelation for a moment bemused Ojuka. He shook his head, dazed. He fought his incredulity, for this was true, it was happening now, and it could bring his death. But, for all that – 'For a village squabble? You bed with me, and follow me, to betray me for a village squabble?' He started to chuckle and then to laugh. It was insane, and yet it was deadly sanity of the most ancient and blood-letting kind. It was true, it was so. 'Then you have *earned* my head, Kutunda . . . '

Kutunda's black face became a mask, as Ojuka's black face creased into high-pitched laughter.

Cowley and Murphy, speeding to the Ashcroft Hotel, kept in touch with Bodie, watching Avery's house.

When Bodie answered, he said: 'Three seven . . . Alone and palely loitering . . . '

Cowley, on the R/T said: 'John Keats, at this hour. You surprise me, Bodie.'

'I do my best. Where are you?'

'About ten miles from the hotel, and I intend to escort Colonel Ojuka to his conference personally, if I have to. Anything moving there?'

'One visitor, just now. Still in the house. And you're going to like this bit. He's African.'

'Is he now. It's beginning to fit, then. Avery and the Colonel's wife met last night. So stay put, and keep your eyes open. If either one of them shows, I want to know about it. Out.'

He half-turned and said to Murphy: 'Now let's give four five his early morning call. Alpha to four five, come in, four five.'

George Cowley, chief of CI5, spent some time in calling over the R/T for one of his ace agents, four five, alias Ray Doyle. But he did not receive an answer.

The answer became partially apparent when Cowley's car drew up on the forecourt of the hotel among a clutter of ambulances and police cars and officialdom. It did not take long for Cowley to put the picture together, and he did not like what he saw. He called Bodie.

'We're a jump behind them, Bodie. They've taken Ojuka, and Doyle with him, shot a girl at the hotel –'

Bodie said, sharply: 'What about Doyle?'

'Disarmed. But not dead. At least – not when they left.'

Parker was saying in a sneering tone: 'So you're CI5, are you? You've got quite a reputation. If we get a little time together, I'm going to find out just what makes you tick.'

'Like,' said Doyle, his hands bound at his back, 'you did with that girl back there? You're a very brave man, aren't you – with your mouth.'

Parker's smile was that of a killer who looks forward to his work. He backhanded Doyle across the mouth.

Doyle's head snapped back and his tousled hair flew up. But he gave Parker no satisfaction from the blow.

At Doyle's back his hands were working away, tunnelling into the crevice in the upholstery of the car's seating between seat and back. He found a small hard object, and as his fingers closed over it, feeling the shape, he knew he had in his hands one of those little disposable cigarette lighters . . .

Doyle eyed Parker, and the gun, and the heavy in the driving seat, for they'd changed places to let Parker have a little fun with the prisoner; and Ray Doyle began to turn the lighter around, and get it set, ready to flick it into light.

If the thing was not empty . . .

The two kidnap cars whirled along country roads and soon slowed and turned into the driveway between brick pillars leading up to Avery's house.

Snug in the bushes, Bodie focussed his binoculars on the cars as they halted. The doors opened. Bodie drew in a quick hissing breath. Ray Doyle was bundled from the car, handled roughly, dragged along and up the steps into the house. His hands were bound behind his back. He looked dishevelled.

Bodie controlled himself, lowered the glasses and flicked his R/T on. He spoke curtly.

'Three seven to Alpha. They're here. Two cars. The lady's with them. But no sign of Avery.'

Cowley's reply came over the air from his car as it hurtled on towards the scene of the coming action.

'We're on our way, three seven. My guess is that Avery will pick them up before he runs, so stay close. But I want no action until we get there.'

Bodie sounded mutinous.

'What if they move? That's Doyle in there . . . '

'I'll have no heroics on Doyle's behalf.' Cowley was grim and contained, fighting himself as much as imposing his authority on Bodie. They both knew the score here. 'Is that clear?'

In a most sour tone, Bodie said: 'Yes, sir.'

Ray Doyle was being taken down dark steps into a deep cellar, with old brick walls and racks, and a dusty musty floor of stone slabs. Parker slammed him down. Doyle thumped rib-crushingly against the wall. The smell of the place got up his nose.

'You put up quite a little show for yourself, didn't you?' said Parker.

He gloated on Doyle, hard, vicious, the killer in charge.

Doyle looked at the damage he'd done to Parker, the beginning purpling of the bruises.

'Was a pleasure – '

The rock-hard fist slammed into Doyle's guts. Parker panted with the force of the blow.

'Yeah? How is it now?'

Parker hit Doyle again. He stood over the CI5 agent, contemplating his work with satisfaction plastered over his ugly bruised face.

'*My* pleasure, hard man. You take it easy there and think.' Parker turned away, rubbing his knuckles. 'Think about what you got coming next.'

He went out and the sound of the lock clicking over was like the sound of the iron gates of the Bastille clanging shut.

Painfully, Doyle shoved himself up right against the

angle of wall. His guts were on fire. But there was no time to hang around feeling sorry for himself.

His fingers uncurled from their vice-like grip. The little transparent disposable lighter felt like the keys to Heaven. He turned the thing the right way up, got a good grip on it, and flicked the wheel . . .

Upstairs in Avery's house Ojuka was menaced by the guns of Moon and Davis.

Kutunda sat dispassionately to one side, eyeing her husband as the authoritative voice of Faroud boomed in the study. Avery had a nice house. But no one was taking any notice of the furnishings right now.

Faroud's heavy form dominated Ojuka.

'So, Colonel. It would seem that you are to miss your conference after all. Thanks to your good lady here.'

Ojuka spoke evenly.

'We are still a long way from Betan, Faroud.' His dark eyes glanced with contempt at Parker's henchmen. 'And you have no allies here but these jackals.'

'Oh, we are not so far. The government that so kindly provided these men has a ship waiting for us at sea. And the British Government's own Mister Avery will shortly take us to it.' Faroud's heavy face broke into a mocking smile. 'Your enemies are all around you, Colonel. Even in this civilised land.'

Ojuka's teeth showed. But the smile was ironical, like that of a barracuda discussing mealtime.

'And you? What will you do, Faroud? Will you run to your master's heels again? Or crawl into some corner, like the vermin that you are?'

The insult registered with Faroud. But he bit back his immediate anger, for he was in command, and he held the power . . .

'I shall accompany you, Colonel, to ensure that you arrive in Betan alive, and in one piece, for a short time, at least. And when the crowds are gathered, I shall wield the sword that takes your head from off your body, and there will be no more Ojuka to trouble the people's conscience in Betan.'

The promise was there, hanging blood-red between them. The bright blade uplifted, the hushed murmur of the crowds, the sunshine and the heat and the flies. And then the swift lethal descent of the blade, the silver stained a ghastly hue, the tumbling roll of the head, and the beast roar of the crowd . . . It was all there, in that quiet room of an English country house . . .

Parker walked in. He was still rubbing his knuckles and he looked brisk.

'All right. Let's get set. Avery's on his way.'

Now they could all hear the sound of a helicopter, rising as the chopper swung about to make a neat landing close to the house. The whirlwind from the blades flattened bushes and drove leaves scuttering. Bodie pulled his impact of steel-jacketed lead.

John Avery, head bent, alighted from the chopper.

Bodie called out on the R/T.

'Three seven to Alpha. Avery's arrived. Looks like a helicopter pick-up for Ojuka.' Bodie made up his mind. He was well aware what the big white chief had said. He also knew more about Cowley than Cowley suspected. And, making everything else very small in the balance, there was Ray Doyle in that house, with plug-uglies with guns at his head . . .

Bodie spoke with decision, in a way that brooked no argument.

'I'm going in.'

He drew his gun and, crouched over, started for the house.

Cowley grabbed up his own R/T, furious.

'*Stay put*, Bodie! That's an order!'

The R/T remained dead.

Cowley glowered.

He said: 'Insurbordinate – ' And did not finish.

His car screamed around the bends, and the police car he'd ordered to tag on from the hotel had difficulty keeping up.

Suspecting the worst, knowing the balloon had gone up, John Avery wasted no time. He hastily collected papers from his study, stuffing them into a briefcase. He spoke to the others as he worked.

'Parker, you'll come with us.' He nodded at Moon and Davis. 'You've made arrangements for these two?'

'They've been paid. They know what to do.'

'Good. All right, get him outside and you can be on your way.'

Davis and Moon grabbed Ojuka and started to hustle him to the door. The Colonel stopped, and, rather to their surprise, the two henchmen found that they had stopped, too. Ojuka opened his mouth, and Faroud about to follow, halted as Ojuka spoke.

'Avery – what have you gained from this?'

Avery, to everyone's surprise, pondered a moment, before he answered.

'I have a good many interests invested in your African neighbours, Colonel. In return for you, they will be safeguarded against the foreseeable future. And Betan has agreed to do the same for them; when you are – er – satisfactorily dealt with, in their eyes.'

The government man let his glance rest for a moment on Katunda, sitting so quietly like a black pillar of doom in that comfortable study.

'I might add,' Avery concluded, 'that your own colourful history provided us with a very willing source of information on you.'

Ojuka looked at them, looked at them as he might look at what crawled out of rotten meat in the heat of his own land.

'She has a belief. You are like this scum. All you have is a price.'

Avery winced as Parker, moving swiftly forward, slashed Ojuka with the back of his hand. The black Colonel's head lolled and he sagged in the grip of the two henchmen.

Parker stabbed a finger at Ojuka.

'There'll be a lot more of that for you, I promise you . . . ' He fairly snarled at his men. 'Get him out.'

Avery shook himself as though from an incipient bad

dream. As Ojuka was forcibly hustled from the study, Avery resumed packing his briefcase.

'All right,' he said, stuffing in the last papers and closing the lid and snapping the locks. 'Let's go.' Then, with a touch of ironic courtesy, he looked at Kutunda, and finished: 'Madame.'

Kutunda rose with the graceful movement. She was not touched by what this man thought of her.

'What of the other one?'

Faroud started. Surprised, he turned a questioning look on Parker. The ugly face returned his look with a hard contemptuous gaze.

'Other One?' said Faroud.

'One of his CI5 bodyguards. We brought him along –'

Avery cut in, shocked.

'You've got him here?' At Parker's nod, Avery rasped out: 'Then kill him. Get rid of him.'

Parker said: 'Those two'll get rid of him. I'll put him out now.'

He went towards the back and the cellar door as the others exited by the front. The helicopter waited. The group headed for it.

From his vantage point in the bushes Bodie spotted them. He spotted them all – except the one person he wanted to see. Bodie frowned, about to make a break for it and halted by the appearance of this mob of people, he hung on for a space yet.

'Bring him out, you bastards,' he said to himself. 'Bring him out!'

Parker clattered down the steps, gun in hand, thinking pleasurable thoughts about what he was going to do with this interfering monkey from CI5.

Doyle heard him coming.

The lighter had not been empty.

The flame had licked up as the wheel spun. The flame had burned through the ropes binding him. Also, the flame had burned through a quantity of Doyle's skin, and he could feel the scorching pain of that, the sweat thick on

115

his forehead. His hair was a ruffled bird's nest and he was mad clean through.

Parker crashed the door open, gloating upon his intending victim.

'We're leaving,' he said, and levelled the automatic in the aim, ready to give Doyle his quietus. 'So here's yours, hard man – '

The last strand of rope parted and Doyle heaved up like a spectre from a grave. Parker yelped in surprise and as Doyle whipped the gun away tightened on the trigger. The auto blasted shots at the ceiling.

And then Ray Doyle took Parker to pieces.

Outside, waiting, jittering, Bodie heard the shot and waited for no more. He was on his feet and running like a maniac for the house.

The pilot of the chopper waiting for his passengers spotted the fleeting frantic figure of Bodie. The pilot did not hesitate, surprised though he was. He pulled his gun, leaned from the canopy, and opened fire on Bodie.

Bullets ripped into the gravel before Bodie's feet.

He dived and rolled and came up in the aim and shot at the chopper. Bullets pranged. But the group around Ojuka and Avery scattered and now the henchmen were shooting at Bodie. Gunfire broke shatteringly against the sky.

Bodie was caught in a cross-fire. He broke for cover and hunkered down as leaves split and spun away under the impact of steel-jacketed lead.

He took careful aim at the helicopter and put one into the pilot before rolling away and avoiding a blast from Avery's group. Some of them had broken for the parked cars. But some were still shooting back . . .

Ray Doyle crashed from the house entrance, aiming Parker's auto, re-loaded, shot out Moon who was still trying to deal with Ojuka. Davis swivelled to meet Doyle's devastating appearance. He shot as Doyle whipped away and Bodie saw the exposed flank and did not hesitate. Bodie shot and it was goodbye Davis.

Faroud splattered the ground around Bodie and the CI5

man was forced to dive recklessly for cover again. At that a bullet punched a hole in his coat, whereat Master Bodie voiced a trenchant opinion.

But that movement freed Doyle again. In a series of the old One-Two they'd dealt with the opposition, and now Doyle put two into Faroud. The big heavy-set man did not go down over-fast; but he went down under the impact of the slugs from Parker's auto – the same auto that had shot bullets into the pretty receptionist.

Cowley's car and the following police car rolled up the drive as Bodie and Doyle, the Bisto Kids, sprang to their feet and closed in on Avery and Kutunda.

Avery lay on the gravel, shaking, still clutching his briefcase.

Kutunda stood as she had stood in the carpark when, with her information, gunmen had tried to take her husband away that first time.

Bodie said to Avery, and the gun spoke as eloquently: 'On your feet!'

Avery stood up. Doyle fancied he could hear the fellow's teeth chattering. But after the smacking uproar of concentrated gunfire the old ears were not, for a time, as sensitive as they should be. The partners looked at Avery and Kutunda, and now they did not care overmuch for what they saw.

From the shelter of one of the cars, where his expertise in self-preservation had taken him, Colonel Ojuka emerged. He advanced on Bodie and Doyle, and he did not – at first – look at Avery or Kutunda.

Ojuka looked upon the carnage. He saw the dead bodies. He smelled the blood.

Colonel Ojuka beamed.

'Excellent,' he said, and his nostrils widened. 'Excellent!'

Murphy was out of the car and across to Ojuka. He started to untie the Colonel's bonds.

The police from the following car converged on Avery and Kutunda. Bodie and Doyle were surrounded, suddenly, by bustle. And then, like Jove preceded by his

117

thunderbolts, George Cowley confronted them.

Cowley looked at Bodie. Bodie looked at a point in space somewhere over Cowley's left shoulder. Bodie's lips pushed together.

Cowley said: 'You disobeyed an order, Bodie. I told you to stay put.'

'Yes, sir.' Bodie's tone, casual perhaps, light, yet matter-of-fact and to the point, was all Bodie. 'Couldn't let them get away, though, could I?' He nodded that sleek dark head of his at Doyle and Ojuka. 'Think how you'd feel if we'd lost him . . . '

Cowley lowered his eyebrows, looking hard at Bodie.

'My concern for Ojuka has nothing to do with insubordination, Bodie.'

Bodie was looking at Doyle.

'Who said anything about Ojuka, sir?'

Before Cowley could get a suitable reply together, Ojuka, rubbing his wrists, still beaming, joined them.

'Well, my friend. You have come to escort me to the conference, yes?'

Faced with such a sublime confidence, all Cowley could do was graciously acquiesce. He nodded, briefly.

'Certainly, Colonel. We may be ten minutes late; but under the circumstances, I think our people will understand.'

'Then let us delay no longer.' Ojuka moved his shoulders, building back to full form. He moved off with Cowley and then spoke to the partners. 'You fight well, gentlemen. I shall remember you for it.'

Then he went with Cowley to the Rover and the partners saw him driven swiftly away.

But Colonel Ojuka had not left before he had exchanged a long wordless look with Kutunda . . .

Bodie and Doyle stood together.

In all the action Doyle had ignored the pain in his wrists. Now he became aware of the smarting sting where the little disposable lighter's flame had licked him.

'Well,' said Doyle, with that typical Doyleish throaty

half-laugh bubbling in his words. 'There goes my violin practice for a couple of weeks.'

'Yeah?' said Bodie, the hard man. 'Too bad.'

He was watching the face of Kutunda, at the rear window of the police car as it disappeared along the drive.

'Some woman. I wonder what the other three were like?'

Still nursing his wrists, Doyle followed his partner's gaze. 'Don't know.'

The car at last vanished, the silence dropped down, soon the ambulances would be here for the corpses. Avery was for the chop. Ojuka would try to get the backing he needed. It was just another wrapped-up case for the agents of CI5, the Big A, the Squad.

Doyle did not rub his wrists. He'd have a word with the ambulance boys when they got here, get something to put on, help soothe the sting.

'But,' said Doyle. 'I imagine Ojuka feels like I do right now . . .'

Bodie raised his left eyebrow. 'How's that?'

'He ought to be more careful about who he gets tied up with . . .'

Bodie looked at Doyle, and Doyle looked at Bodie, and then they set about clearing up the mess.

TRAVERSE OF THE GODS

by Bob Langley

The Eiger, 1944 – In a desperate attempt to
turn defeat into victory, German and American
mountaineers are locked in an appalling
struggle on the notorious North Wall of
Europe's deadliest mountain – a struggle with
vital implications for the development of the
atomic bomb.

'Brilliant . . . in a class by itself'
Jack Higgins

'Written in the best adventure tradition'
Publishers Weekly

ADVENTURE/THRILLER   0 7221 5410 0   £1.50

And don't miss Bob Langley's other exciting thrillers:
DEATH STALK
WAR OF THE RUNNING FOX
WARLORDS
– also available in Sphere Books

HITLER'S SEED LIVES ON . . .

THE WATCHDOGS OF ABADDON

IB MELCHIOR

1945:

A group of SS officers flees in mortal terror from a remote hut in the heart of Nazi Germany. In their wake, a trail of bloody carnage – and in their keeping a secret prized possession: *the son of Adolf Hitler*.

1978:

A motiveless murder, a single photograph and an instinct for trouble plunge Harry Bendicks, ace investigator, into a nightmare world of political intrigue, frenzied murder and power-crazed manipulation. The trail leads Bendicks back 30 years to war-torn Europe and the deadly horror of a lethal conspiracy which threatens to destroy the very fabric of the Western world.

THE WATCHDOGS HAVE WOKEN – AND THEY HERALD THE FOURTH REICH!

THE WATCHDOGS OF ABADDON blazes a trail from Nazi Germany to the heart of Washington, and to the fabulous wealth of the Middle Eastern oil empires, and explodes in a brilliant, nerve-shattering climax of devastating evil.

ADVENTURE THRILLER   0 7221 6023 2   £1.75

I, SAID THE SPY

by Derek Lambert

Fact: Each year a nucleus of the wealthiest and most influential members of the Western world meet to discuss the future of the world's superpowers at a secret conference called Bilderberg.

A glamorous millionairess just sighting loneliness from the foothills of middle-age . . . a French industrialist whose wealth matches his masochism and meanness . . . a whizz-kid of the seventies conducting a life-long love affair with diamonds, these are just three of the Bilderbergers who have grown to confuse position with invulnerability. A mistake which could prove lethal when a crazed assassin is on the loose . . . a journalist dedicated to exposing the conference infiltrates their midst . . . and intelligence agents from Moscow, Washington and London penetrate Bilderberg's defences to reveal a conspiracy of mind-boggling proportions . . .

I, SAID THE SPY is a novel on a grand scale which sweeps the reader along on a wave of all-out excitement and suspense until the final stunning climax.

ADVENTURE/THRILLER   0 7221 5346 5   £1.75

JOE POYER

TUNNEL WAR

POLITICAL DYNAMITE!

In 1911 Europe was rushing headlong towards world war. And beneath the English Channel a massive tunnel was already under construction. When fire wreaked havoc in an unfinished tunnel shaft, James Bannerman, the project chief, smelt trouble. Further deadly 'accidents' confirmed his suspicions – the project was being systematically destroyed by a team of professional saboteurs.

Bannerman already faced an impossible choice: sacrifice the tunnel – or the lives of his men. But nothing had quite prepared him for the devastating web of murder and conspiracy that stretched from Ireland to Germany to the heart of Britain's political arena and which threatened to destroy everything he'd ever fought for – including his life . . .

ADVENTURE THRILLER   0 7221 7027 0   £1.50

And, don't miss Joe Poyer's other thrilling novels, also available in Sphere Books:

THE DAY OF RECKONING
OPERATION MALACCA
THE BALKAN ASSIGNMENT
THE CHINESE AGENDA
NORTH CAPE
HELL SHOT
THE CONTRACT

A selection of bestsellers from SPHERE

FICTION

SEA LEOPARD	Craig Thomas	£1.95 ☐
BLOOD RED WINE	Laurence Delaney	£2.25 ☐
MUSIC FOR CHAMELEONS	Truman Capote	£1.50 ☐
TRAVERSE OF THE GODS	Bob Langley	£1.50 ☐
THE RING	Danielle Steel	£1.75 ☐

FILM & TV TIE-INS

FORT APACHE, THE BRONX	Heywood Gould	£1.75 ☐
BARRIERS	William Corlett	£1.00 ☐
THE GENTLE TOUCH	Terence Feely	£1.25 ☐
ON THE LINE	Anthony Minghella	£1.25 ☐

NON-FICTION

WHAT THIS KATIE DID	Katie Boyle	£1.75 ☐
MICHELLE REMEMBERS	Michelle Smith & Dr Lawrence Padzer	£1.75 ☐
GET FIT FOR LIFE	Henry Cooper	£1.25 ☐
MY STORY	Ingrid Bergman	£1.95 ☐

All Sphere books are available at your local bookshop or newsagent, or can be ordered direct from the publisher. Just tick the titles you want and fill in the form below.

Name _____

Address _____

_____

Write to Sphere Books, Cash Sales Department, P.O. Box 11, Falmouth, Cornwall TR10 9EN

Please enclose cheque or postal order to the value of the cover price plus:

UK: 45p for the first book, 20p for the second and 14p per copy for each additional book ordered to a maximum charge of £1.63

OVERSEAS: 75p for the first book and 21p for each additional book

BFPO & EIRE: 45p for the first book, 20p for the second book plus 14p per copy for the next 7 books, thereafter 8p per book.

Sphere Books reserve the right to show new retail prices on covers which may differ from those previously advertised in the text or elsewhere, and to increase postal rates in accordance with the PO.